Growing up in Penny's Creek

Jen
Hope you enjoy my book, thank you for taking care of Piper she was visiting with you and Jake all those times. Enjoy your time in Penny's Creek

Bobby St. John
Bobby St. John

Fulton Books
Meadville, PA

Published by Fulton Books 2022

ISBN 978-1-63985-792-0 (paperback)
ISBN 978-1-63985-793-7 (digital)

Printed in the United States of America

TO MY "EVERY OTHER TUESDAY" writing group, thank you for your input, advice, and push to keep me writing. You will always be my inspiration.

Chapter 1

IT WAS EARLY MAY in 1982 when Skinny Vinny found the $20 bill in the vacant lot on Edison Road. We were playing whiffle ball when Vinny spotted it next to a small gray rock. Now $20 these days isn't a whole lot, but back in '82, it was a huge find to a thirteen-year-old. Even a dollar was big. With a dollar, you get a Superman comic, a Snickers candy bar, and a Pepsi. What else was there in life! Well, besides girls and horror movies, but we'll talk about that later.

Anyway, Vinny started to do the dancing jig he did whenever he was happy. He called it the Catalano Jig. Vinny Catalano was also the craziest mother I knew. "Twenty bucks, Morgan. We're rich," he shouted at me.

"I don't think we're rich," I told him. "But we're going to have a kick ass week at least." My brain began to think of the ways we could spend it.

"Let's go to the CCC," my friend suggested. I agreed, and we picked up the whiffle bat and ball and headed into town. I lived in Penny's Creek, Connecticut. It was a small town on the Connecticut River. The population was about ten thousand.

Though it was a small town, we had everything one would need. There were Nelson's groceries; a bank; the Nail It Hardware store; a unisex hairdresser; the CCC, which stood for Comics, Candy, and Cards; two restaurants, not including the McDonald's and the doughnut shop; two clothing stores; Sully's Pub; Pete's Gas Station and Bait Shop; a Texaco; a flower shop; two banks; and the Merritt movie theatre that had two huge screens.

In addition, Penny's Creek had a police station, where the father of my friend, Sara, was the chief; the doctor husband-and-wife-team of Mark and Mindy Smith, the elementary school that went from kindergarten to eighth grade, the volunteer fireman station, and the library/town hall.

Vinny kept doing his Catalano Jig as we walked down Elm Street. Vinny was a tall thirteen-year-old and was nicknamed Skinny Vinny because he was thin like Olive Oil from the *Popeye* cartoons. He was tall and lanky and probably weighed just much as me, and I was five inches shorter with dark curly hair. He had straight brown hair and a big nose he wasn't fond of. As I said before, he was crazy but a good crazy. He did insane stunts on his bike, acted like a nutcase in public sometimes, and would hit on any pretty girl he met no matter the age. But he was one of my best friends and the sweetest kid I knew. He was nice to everyone as well. Well, except to the town bullies, Tim White and his jerk friends, Lucas and Fat Willy.

"Too bad, Andy is visiting his Grandma." I grinned. "Otherwise, we would have to split the twenty with him too."

As we turned on Main Street, we heard the police siren and watched Sheriff Foster roar off in his brown cruiser toward the east end of town.

"Wonder what's up," Vinny said.

I shrugged, and we walked on another three hundred feet and entered the CCC; The Comics, Candy, and Card shop was run by Artie Lombard and his cousin, Tika.

Tika was one of the three best-looking girls I knew. She was nineteen and had light reddish-orange hair and the greatest freckles I ever saw on a girl. I was just learning about breasts, and I was very sure she had some magnificent ones.

She was behind the counter, smoking a cigarette and glancing through a *Captain America* comic book. Rick Springfield's "Jessie's Girl" was playing on the radio behind her. Behind her were racks of any candy you could think of: Milky Way, Big League Chew, Snickers, Reggie Jackson, Good and Plenty, Nerds, M&M's, and tons more. On the right side of the shop were the shelves of comics, old and new—*Justice League of America, Ironman, Adventure Comics, Archie and Jughead, The Flash, Wonder Woman, Uncanny X-men,* and *Spiderman.* On the left side where the display stands of baseball and football cards.

Tika looked up as we walked up to her. "What's up, dirtbags?" she grinned.

"Hello, my beautiful darling," Vinny said, clutching his chest. "You make my heart flutter."

"Dumbass," I muttered. Vinny had been in love with Tika Murphy ever since she moved into town three years ago, but who could blame him? She was beautiful, funny, sweet, and loved comic books.

Tika rolled her hazel green eyes and groaned. "You guys are a day early. The new comics come tomorrow."

"Oh," I said, forgetting that. "We'll get a few candy bars instead."

Another police siren sounded past the shop.

Tika nodded her head toward the door. "I just heard from Deputy Duva that another one is missing."

Vinny and I looked at each other in disbelief. In the last two months, two kids had gone missing from Penny's Creek. No traces of them had been found. It was believed that they were kidnapped, but no ransom has come as of yet.

"You guys be sure to not go anywhere alone," Tika said as she rang up two Hershey's bars and Pepsi cans we picked out.

"No sweat, my love," Vinny said, handing her the twenty.

"I'm serious, Vinny and Morgan," Tika said with a hard stare at both of us. "Promise me you guys don't go anywhere alone. The same goes for Andy and Sara."

I nodded. "We promise Tika. See you tomorrow."

Vinny received his change and blew a kiss to Tika, and we left the shop. It was about 5:00 p.m., and both of us had to get home for dinner. I lived about a half mile from downtown on Chestnut Street. My house was a brick Colonial with four bedrooms and two full baths. My parents were pretty well off. My dad was an accountant over in Hartford, and my mom was an English teacher at the Catholic high school over in St. John's Bay, the town next door to us.

Vinny took a look at my overgrown lawn and patted my back. "You best get the lawn cut by Friday," Vinny warned me. "Or your dad will ground you for sure on Saturday."

"I'll do it after dinner tomorrow," I told him.

My friends and I were planning to see John Carpenter's *The Thing* at the Merritt, Saturday afternoon. Tika had agreed to go with us so we could get into the R-rated picture.

"Well, Mom has supper ready, Morgan. I'll see you in school tomorrow. Just think, two more weeks and we are done for the summer." He walked off rubbing the front pocket of his jeans, making sure the money was still there.

Vinny lived three streets over from me. He lived with his mom on a two-bedroom ranch. His father was killed in Vietnam back in the early part of '72. Even though he was only three at the time, Vinny still says he misses him. Mrs. Catalano was the best Mom of all our friends' Moms. She let us stay up late when we slept over and had no curfew in the summertime. She was a waitress over at Sully's Pub.

I walked up the front steps, almost not seeing the blue pickup truck in the driveway behind my mom's station wagon. It was the truck of my older brother, Tom. I forgot that he and his wife, Brett, were coming for dinner.

I smiled. Brett O'Riely was another one of the three most beautiful girls in my life. If you thought Tika was a knockout, then Brett was a goddess among goddesses. She had curly blond hair, light blue eyes, and had the best legs I've ever seen, except for Kathleen Turner's but that was only on TV. She was super cool, and I always wondered why she married a jerk like Tom. But I was thankful she did because I would've never known her then.

Mom was cooking meatloaf in the kitchen while my dad and brother were in the den, watching the news regarding President Regan's health. I still couldn't believe he had been shot. "Hey, shrimp," my brother said, giving me the finger.

"Get that lawn mowed!" my dad hollered.

I grunted and headed up the steps to my bedroom and almost ran into Brett.

"Hey, Morg," she said with a huge smile. She gave me a hug and a kiss on my cheek. "How's my favorite guy?"

"Same old stuff." I blushed. If I died at that moment, I would have been happy. Anytime I was near Brett, my heart would skip a few beats.

"Play you in Space Invaders."

I agreed. Ever since I got my Atari 2600, Brett and I have been having an ongoing contest to get the highest score in Pac-Man, Pitfall, and Space Invaders. So far, I was winning in Space Invaders. Minutes later, we were lying on my *Empire Strikes Back* rug, saving the earth from the alien space ships.

"How's school?" Brett asked. She was lying on my bed as I sat beside her on the floor.

"Getting down to the last few weeks," I said. "I think even the teachers are getting burnt out."

Brett nodded, understanding. She sometimes subbed for the lower grades. On the side, she was working on a novel about a family that gets lost in the Appalachian Mountains. I've read some of her short stories, and I thought they were really good. I wished I was talented like her.

"Tika's getting you guys into the new Carpenter movie?" she asked and swore as enemy spaceship destroyed hers.

"Yep, I can't wait," I said. Tika was Brett's best friend, even though Brett was four years older than her.

"Lucky. Tom hates horror movies. Big wuss." she laughed.

I smiled in agreement.

During dinner, Tom told the family he was going to LA for two weeks on business. He asked me to help Brett around the yard, for which he would pay me $40. I happily agreed. With Vinny's $20 find and this additional $40, I was going to have a great summer.

Chapter 2

I WAS TAKING MY AMERICAN history book out of my locker the next morning when Sara Foster came up to me. She had on a Smurfette T-shirt.

"It was Ben Jackson," she said.

"Who?" I asked, not knowing what she was talking about.

"The kid who has gone missing," she said. "That albino kid from the third grade."

"Oh," I muttered. I closed the locker and began to walk down the hall with my friend.

"Dad says there is no trace of him," she said. "This is getting real bad, Morgan."

Sara was right. Our little town of Penny's Creek was becoming dangerous. Sara always had the inside scoop since she was the sheriff's kid. Plus, Sara was the most curious person I knew. She was very good at finding out what she wanted to know.

Sara was a tomboy/girly girl, if that makes any sense. My dark curly-haired friend loved to play baseball, go fishing, camp out, and launch off firecrackers. But there were other times she would wear dresses and hang out downtown with Jessica Finch, flirting with the high school boys. She had a bigger comic book collection than Vinny and I, consisting mainly of the *Justice League of America, The Flash, The Avengers, and Wonder Woman*. Sara had a beat-up mountain bike as well as china dolls from all over the world.

She had a younger sister in kindergarten that she adored. Since Sara was so good with little kids, she got various babysitting gigs around town. She always had money and was willing to share it with us.

"I babysat him a few times," she said. "He's a cutie. His parents are beside themselves." She paused by the water fountain and took a drink.

"My dad said he was out playing in his backyard after school. His mom was inside doing laundry or something. All she heard was him screaming, and by the time she ran outside, he was gone."

"This is getting really freaky," I said. I didn't tell her I was getting a little scared myself. All my life I thought I was safe, but if a few kids started to disappear, was I safe? Was I so different from them?

Suddenly, I felt someone give me a shove in the back, and I stumbled into Sara. We both turned to see Skinny Vinny standing there grinning.

"Howdy," he said.

"Asshole," Sara and I said at the same time.

"Hey, dollface. I expect foul language from this Irish lad here," Vinny said, putting his left arm over Sara Foster. "But you..."

Sara elbowed him in the stomach. "Watch it you, bony jerk." she grinned.

"You guys see *Different Strokes* last night?" Vinny asked as we walked onto history class.

At 3:00 p.m., I was riding home on my Huffy with Andy Donahue on his. As I said before, Andy was the last member of our quartet. He was Irish, like me, and the tallest in our group. He was opinionated, loved to get you into trouble, and an asshole at times. I loved the guy.

He had four older brothers that would beat him up from time to time, so he would take it out on Vinny and me and sometimes, Parley Whitmore, another kid who hung out with us. He would hold our heads under the pool water or cover us with a huge blanket almost suffocating us. He liked to call it "cooking." Andy also knew more about sex, music, and sports than anyone I knew, thanks to his brothers and sister.

"I'm going to kill Fat Willy when I see him next," Andy said, avoiding a dead squirrel in the street.

Fat Wily had thrown a Hostess CupCake at Andy at lunchtime. Willy usually didn't start trouble without his cronies, Tim and Lucas. That's why Andy was mad. He could take Willy in a fight alone.

"Well," I told him. "Just forget it. He will run off and cry to Tim, and then, we will all be dead meat."

Andy grunted and adjusted his St. Louis Cardinals hat. He had been wearing it for half a year now ever since they beat the Brewers in the World Series. He wasn't even a Cardinal fan.

I was born and raised a Yankee fan and couldn't fathom how anyone couldn't love them. Luckily, my family was all Yankee fans, including 90 percent of the town.

As we turned down Chestnut Street, we saw a tall man with long gray hair. He was standing in the middle of the street. He was dressed only in camouflaged pants and held a large stick.

"Yikes," Andy muttered as we stopped our bikes. "Haywire."

Haywire was the town crazy. He lived in a shack in the woods behind old man Jenkins's place. "The woods are dark like his soul!" he yelled at us.

Haywire was usually harmless and would, once in a while, get thrown in jail by Sheriff Foster for disorderly conduct. No one knew his real name. Dad said Haywire had been living in Penny's Creek for at least forty-five years.

"Hey, Haywire," I called out, looking at him. I noticed a few scratches on his shoulders and chest, and they were bleeding.

Haywire answered by spitting on the ground. "Beware!" he shouted and ran off past a yellow house and into a nearby field.

"The man is off his rocker," Andy said.

We pedaled onto Andy's house on the east end of town. He was going to change his Hostess CupCake smeared T-shirt for his new Joan Jett one. His house was a huge colonial with an inground pool in the back.

I sat on my bike by the mailbox as he ran inside. Nearby, a guy in red shorts was mowing his lawn, showing his butt crack to the neighbors. It was a sunny afternoon with a slight breeze. Overhead, I watched a blue jay land on the tall oak tree in Donahue's front yard. I didn't hear them till they rode up beside me.

"Well, look it here. Its short stuff, wearing his *Aquaman* backpack," a sinister voice stated.

I looked to the left of me and saw Tim White and Lucas Miller on their bikes, glaring at me. Behind him, I heard the heavy breathing of Fat Willy.

"Tim," I said, nodding my head. I looked toward the house, but Andy was still inside. None of his brothers were around either.

Tim White was fifteen. He had been held back twice in grammar school. He was about five feet nine inches and muscular and bore a crew cut. On the left side of his face was a small scar from a knife fight he claimed he got into.

Lucas was one of three only black kids in our school. He had a crooked smile and always wore jeans even on the hottest summer days. His long hair hung just past his shoulders. Lucas was one of the smartest kids at school. I often wondered why he hung out with Tim and Fat Willy. If it makes any sense, Lucas was the nicest of the three of them.

Fat Willy was the fattest kid I knew. His clothes were always covered in whatever food he had been eating that day. He had to be close to two hundred pounds and was only thirteen. His whole family was fat, including his stupid older sister who was just as mean as he was. He had just finished his last bite of a Hostess Cupcake.

"Willy tells me your pal Donahue is talking crap about us," Tim growled.

My heart beat a little faster. *Come on, Andy. Hurry the hell up.*

I looked down at my shoes, avoiding Tim's cold eyes. "Don't believe everything Willy tells you."

"You call me a liar, O'Riely?"

"I saw you throw the cupcake, Willy," I said, getting annoyed.

"I say we kick his ass," Lucas said, slapping a fly of his jeans.

My hand slowly reached down to the water bottle on my bike. "I rather you didn't," I said softly. Andy was still taking his sweet ass time. Probably sitting on the throne, reading a *Betty and Veronica* comic book.

13

"We rather we did," Tim growled, reaching to grab onto my arm.

I held up the water bottle in my hand and squeezed. Water shot directly into Tim's eyes, blinding him for a few seconds.

Then, I took off pedaling as fast I could down Chestnut Street. Out of the corner of my eyes, I saw Andy standing on his doorstep, watching as the three bullies chased after me. "Move it, Morgan!" my friend yelled.

I was a pretty good bike rider and knew I definitely could out-ride Willy, but Lucas and Tim were in good shape and were gaining fast. I quickly passed the guy with his butt crack showing and hoped he would yell at the trio to leave me alone. He just kept mowing.

"You are so dead, O'Riely!" Tim shouted.

My mind worked like sixty, trying to form a plan of escape. If I headed downtown, there would be many pedestrians. But downtown was a good mile away. If I headed over to the woods, I could run and hide in them. But even then, they may reach me in time.

I pedaled even faster and almost wiped out on the curb to hop onto the sidewalk. I looked over at my shoulder and saw Lucas only a few feet behind me. I'm so dead.

I quickly swerved to the left, and Lucas shot past me. I looked back over my shoulder at Tim, who was now just a few feet behind. Fat Willy had come to a complete stop on the side of the road, leaning on his handlebars. I hoped he was having a heart attack.

Tim grinned evilly as his front tire hit the back of mine. My teeth clamped together as I fought my bike from wobbling. Tim swore as I kept my bike upright.

"Eat me!" I shouted and pedaled for all that I was worth. But unfortunately, Lucas was back at my side, and he shoved me over. I fell off my bike at the end of a driveway, landing on some discarded boxes at the curb.

My chest tightened up, and I tried to breathe, but I couldn't. The wind was knocked out of me. I tried waving my arms up in the air, something my dad told me to do when you had the wind knocked out of you.

Then, Tim and Lucas stood over me, laughing. I saw Tim ready to kick me in the stomach, so I quickly rolled to the left, and instead, he kicked an empty Lite Bright Box.

I sat up and found myself able to breathe again. A dog barked from inside the house behind me.

"Pick him up," Tim ordered Lucas and the newly arrived and breathing heavily Willy. Each one grabbed one of my arms and picked me up. "This is for messing with me," Tim muttered and punched me hard in the stomach. I let out a grunt. Tears filled my eyes.

"You boys leave him be," an elderly woman's voice yelled from the house.

"Shut up, you old bag," Willy shouted back at her. He was sweating like crazy, and some of it was hitting my face.

"Hit him again, Tim." Willy laughed as we heard the door slam close behind us.

Lucas loosened his grip on me. "No. He's had enough, guys."

Tim spit on the ground and glared at Lucas. "I'll say when it's enough, jerk face."

That's when a siren sounded startling all four of us. A police car had pulled over the side of the street next to us. "You boys are causing trouble?" said the sheriff as he stepped out of his cruiser.

Fat Willy and Lucas immediately dropped me, and I fell to my knees. I felt like punching Tim where it counts but decided against it. The cavalry had arrived.

Sheriff Will Foster stood on the sidewalk with his hands on his hips, dressed in his brown police uniform. Sara's father was a big guy. He had to be at least six three, and I always thought he could rip a telephone book in half with his bare hands. Plus, he had, like, the coolest mustache ever, with the exception of the actor Dennis Weaver from *Duel*.

"Why is it I always find you causing trouble, Mr. White?" he asked.

Tim smiled the famous smile he always gave to the teachers at school. The smile that says, "Hey look, I'm an angel."

"We were just roughhousing, Sheriff." He looked over at his friends and glared at me. "Right, guys?"

"Oh sure," Willy said, and he actually helped me to my feet.

"I find that hard to believe, Mr. Palmer," the sheriff said. He looked over at me. "You all right, Morgan?"

I nodded, my heart still racing, but my fear level had dropped. I looked over at Tim's eyes, and I knew I better watch what I say. Otherwise, my hopefully kick ass summer would become one ass-kicking summer. "We are just messing around is all," I told him.

The sheriff nodded. "You boys get off this lady's lawn."

He watched as Tim and his friends walked back to their bikes. "Oh, by the way, Tim," Sheriff Foster said. "You don't know anything about Pete's gas station getting broken into last night, do you?"

Tim stopped short with his back to the policeman. "Uh...no, Sheriff." He looked back and smiled. "Have a nice day."

He then got on his bike and rode away with Lucas and Willy, pedaling hard to keep up.

I, by now, had picked up my bike and was sitting on it. I saw Andy had arrived and was watching me from across the street.

Sheriff Foster stood looking at me for a few seconds. I knew that he knew I was lying. "Okay, Morgan. Get going." he smiled at me.

I nodded and biked over to Andy who had a puzzled look on his face. The sheriff got back into his cruiser. "If you see Sara at the CCC," he called out from the passenger window, "tell her to be home by five thirty"

"Will do, Mr. Foster," Andy said and waved as the police car pulled away.

"What the hell did I miss?" he asked me.

I wanted to rip off his stupid Joan Jett T-shirt he had on. This may have not have happened because of it, but I knew it wasn't Andy's fault. As we biked into town, I told him about my near beating. Andy shook his head. "I'm going to get that fat bum," he said.

We turned down Main Street. Traffic was starting to pick up from people coming home from work. "Let's just hope we can avoid them this summer. That's all I want."

"It's a good thing you didn't sell out Tim or you really would meet his dog."

I shuddered and prayed that I didn't. This past Easter, Tim's father, who was a real jerk but spoiled his son rotten, gave Tim a new dog. It was a full-grown Doberman pinscher named Lucifer. It was a known fact that Lucifer was quite mad and that Tim had trained him to attack on command. No one really saw the dog yet because Tim's dad kept him in the fenced-in backyard, but I wasn't planning on meeting the dog anytime soon. Vinny swore that Lucifer had killed twenty rabbits and a Saint Bernard and had buried them in the backyard. We all believed him.

Chapter 3

WE SAW SARA AND Skinny Vinny standing outside of the CCC shop, waiting for us. Vinny jumped when he saw us and started doing his dancing jig. "You're here, you're here. We're saved!" he shouted.

Sara looked over and shook her head. "Remind me how many times did your mom drop you when you were little?"

Andy had promised not to tell Sara what happened. I didn't want her to think I was chicken. I usually told her everything, but this, I decided to keep to myself. We would tell Vinny later.

"What the hell," Sara said, tapping her Mickey Mouse watch. "Late once again."

"Sorry," I said. "I was just—"

Andy broke in. "I wanted to show you my new T-shirt."

Sara grunted and brushed her curly dark hair out of her eyes. "Pat Benatar is way better."

The four of us entered the shop and found Artie Lombard behind the counter. Artie was overweight, bald, and smoked ten times more than his cousin, Tika. He was one of the coolest adults I knew. He would always credit us if we didn't have enough money and always put aside some of the popular comics for my friends and I.

He was sitting behind the counter with his feet up, reading the newest action comics. "Well, if it's not the Justice League," he said. He pointed at Sara. "Wonder Woman and her three stooges. Two Micks and an Italian Skelton."

"Oh man, you are so funny," Vinny mocked him. "And you're the fattest meatball eating jerk I know."

He walked over to the new comics. "Where is my future wife?"

"Tika went over to get us dinner at Lulu's café," Artie told him. He stood up to ring up a fifth grader who was buying some Yankee cards and a *Flash* comic.

"Hey, Morg, look," Andy whispered, pointing to the back of the store where Artie and Tika had begun to set up some shelves. They planned to start selling board games in the summer. Standing near one of the shelves, drinking a 7-Up, was Kate Sheppard and her friend, Betsey.

"Hommina, hommina, hommina," Vinny said behind me, doing his best Ralph Cramden impersonation.

I just stared at Kate. As I said before, I personally know three of the most beautiful girls ever. Tika, the fiery redhead; Bret, my goddess sister-in-law; and then, there was Kate Sheppard, eighth grader.

Kate, I secretly named the Bronx Beauty, had moved from New York last year. She was tall, but then again, everyone was taller than me; had long, straight dark hair that went a few inches below her shoulders, and big almond-shaped brown eyes. Whenever she smiled at me, all thoughts, breathe, and speaking words would freeze up on me.

"Oh, you guys, give me a break," Sara said. "You do realize your whole lives revolve around comic books, horror movies, and girls."

"What else is there in life?" Vinny, Andy, and I said at the same time.

Sometimes, I thought Sara got jealous when the three of us talked about other girls. Sara was super cute, and I knew a ton of guys that liked her. But she was our good friend, so we really didn't look at her in that way.

"Well, are you going to talk to her, Morgan?" Andy said. "Or wait to grow some balls?"

"If he doesn't do it now...," Tika said, coming up behind me and squeezing my shoulder. I didn't even hear her come into the store. "Then he's not going to the movies with us on Saturday."

"Oh great," I muttered, "an audience."

I walked around the counter and approached the beautiful and sweet Kate Sheppard, not knowing she would go missing in less than two months.

"Hi, Morgan," she said with her heart-melting smile. Kate had this smile that just seemed to always make a person happy. She was super sweet, and even though she had just turned fourteen last month, she had the body of a fifteen-year-old!

I might have said hi. I really don't remember. I do remember leaning against one of the oakwood shelves, and seconds later, three of them came crashing down to the floor. To me, the noise sounded worse than Godzilla walking through a glass factory.

"Real smooth, O'Riely," Artie muttered with his feet back up on the counter. He took a bite out of his hamburger. "You are cleaning that up."

Vinny and Andy howled with laughter as my face turned beet red. Vinny let out an "ooof" as Sara elbowed him in the stomach. Even Betsey was smiling. Betsey was pretty herself, but I always thought she had a mean streak in her.

"Don't worry," Kate said, bending down and helping me put the shelves back up. "I'm clumsy myself. I once dropped a whole plate of cookies my mom had just baked."

I didn't remind her that I was voted the most clumsiness for the last two years in my grade. "Thank you, Kate," I said instead, my nervousness gone. She had that effect on people. She could make anyone feel at ease.

Minutes later, we were all laughing about it and talking about what had happened at school that day. As I was leaving the store with my newest Action comics, *X-Men* and *Aquaman* books, Kate told me she was glad she wasn't the only clumsy one in town.

I walked Sara back to her house. She told me she had something to give me. The Fosters lived in a huge yellow Victorian, right beside Penny's Creek itself. They had a wrap-around, screened-in porch where we hung out when it was raining. Sara's mom was cooking something up delicious when we entered the house. Mrs. Kelly Foster was a small, stout woman who reminded me a little of Mrs. Ingalls from *Little House on the Prairie*. Her hair was usually up in a bun, and she seldom wore anything but dresses. She was a fantastic cook and had a great talent for making clothes.

"Hi, Morgan." She smiled as we entered the kitchen. She wiped her hands on her rose-colored apron and gave me a hug. "How's your mom?"

"She's good," I told her as my eyes discovered the pork chops cooking on the stove. Next to it was some fresh asparagus. *Maybe she will grill it,* I thought. Nothing beats grilled asparagus.

She caught me looking. "You want to stay for dinner?"

"Hell yes, he does." Sara laughed.

"Sara, little ears is upstairs. Shh," her mom said. "I'll call your mom and tell her."

"Come on," Sara said, leading me upstairs. We found her five-year-old sister lying in the middle of the hallway on the plush tan carpet.

"Morgan!" she shouted. Her curly blond hair was matted down from the bath she must have just taken. She was moving her arms and legs in a scissorlike motion.

"Hey, Christy," I said, squatting down beside her. "Watcha doing?"

"Making carpet angles," she said.

I laughed. Damn, that kid was adorable. Sara bent down and rubbed her hair and gave her a quick kiss.

I loved Sara's room. On one wall were a bunch of white shelves that held over forty-plus collections of china dolls. On another wall were posters of Pat Benatar, a unicorn, Wonder Woman, and Darth Vader. On top of her dresser was a ten-gallon fish tank with six tropical fish inside.

Sara opened her walk-in closet and took out a brown bag from it. "When my aunt brought me to Salem Mass last weekend, I found this in a gift shop there." She walked over and sat on her full-size bed beside me and handed me the bag.

I reached inside and pulled out what looked like a circular woven object with a few different colored feathers hanging down from it. In the middle of it were different weaves going into different directions.

"It's called a dream catcher," Sara explained. "According to Native Indian customs, it wards off bad mojo."

She paused and gripped my hand. "And nightmares."

Nightmares, I thought. Only Sara knew about them besides my parents and my brother.

"I figured maybe with it," Sara said softly, "Maybe....maybe she will go away and not ever come back."

She, the one Sara was referring to, was the old woman known as Hazel. A horrible, twisted, and cruel old woman that I had been dreaming about ever since I was six. Sometimes, I would wake up and find her dressed in her ratty nightgown, rocking silently in a rocking chair next to my bed and watching me. If I tried to concentrate and try to wake up, sometimes, she would go away. But sometimes, she wouldn't go away, and that's when the nightmare went real bad.

She would laugh from inside my closet. Small giggles at first, and then, they would turn into something that I can only say was inhuman. She then would slide open the closet door. She would have a nervous twitch, and as she shook her head, saliva would ooze out of her mouth. Her curly snow-white hair was always unkempt, and the six teeth she had were yellow. Hazel would hold up a long chain and would step out from the darkened closet.

"Morg, you there?" I heard Sara ask.

I nodded, coming back to the real world. I looked over and saw the concern on my friend's face. I felt like I was going to cry. Not because I was thinking of the old woman but because of the love I felt for Sara Foster. She was indeed my greatest friend. "Thank you," I whispered.

She put her arm over my shoulder and leaned against me. "You're welcome, pal. We'll beat her yet."

When I got home, I hung Sara's dream catcher on my window. Hazel didn't come to visit me that night.

Chapter 4

SATURDAY MORNING, I WAS up early for two reasons. One was I was excited to see *The Thing* with my pals and the beautiful Tika Murphy.

The other reason was one of the greatest joys in a young person's life—Saturday morning cartoons. Waking up at 8:00 a.m. and curling up on the couch in the den, I would watch *The Super Friends*, followed by the *Smurfs*, then the *Bugs Bunny/Road Runner* show and finally, *Richie Rich*. Nothing beats Batman beating up the Scarecrow, Greedy, Lazy, and Jokey Smurf going on some hike and running into Gargamel; Foghorn Leghorn hitting on the Hens, and Richie playing with all his cool toys.

Vinny came over at ten in time for Bugs, and we ate some pancakes my dad cooked up. Luckily, I mowed the lawn the other day, so my dad was in a good mood. He had told me that there was going to be a town meeting tonight. Mr. Whitmore, the first selectman, wanted to install a curfew. My dad thought it would be a waste of time. All the kids had gone missing in their own backyards during the day.

"Your friend Parley's father is an idiot," he told us.

At eleven thirty, my mom yelled down to us that Tika was out front, waiting. We quickly put on our Chuck Taylors and went outside. Tika was in her red Jeep Wrangler, looking like one of the *Charlie's Angels*. She was wearing jean shorts and NY Yankee T-shirt. Her long curly red hair was tied in a ponytail.

"Hello, Miss America," Vinny said to her, climbing in behind her. I had already called shotgun.

"Don't you ever give up?" she grinned back at him.

"Hey, you're still single," Vinny said. "Fair game in my book."

I always had to give Skinny Vinny credit. The kid had guts. Always went after the girls he wanted. Me? I was a nervous wreck around most of them, especially Kate.

"Hey, Tika," I said, slapping her high five as I got into the passenger seat. "Thanks again for taking us."

"It's what friends do, Morgan," she said. She pulled her Jeep away from the curb and headed down my street. "Next stop, little sis."

Little sis is what Tika called Sara. They were very close. Four years ago, Tika's older sister died from cirrhosis of the liver. I didn't know Tika back then, but I know she took it pretty hard, watching her sister die. Sara, with the exception of Brett, was the closest thing Tika had to a sister now.

The line at the Merritt was pretty long by the time we arrived. Tika, always the smart one, had gotten the tickets for us an hour ago.

"Poor saps," Andy laughed as we walked past the ticket line. Andy had this strut he would do when he thought he was being super cool, which was usually all the time.

We gave Tika our share of the money for the movie tickets. Vinny had paid for mine from the dwindling $20 he had found at the beginning of the week.

Snowcaps and a large Pepsi later, I found myself sitting in between Andy and Sara. Vinny had somehow managed to sit next to Tika. My friend had a strong belief in what a good movie should be. If there wasn't a death or nudity in the first five minutes, then the movie was going to suck. I sometimes found myself following that same belief to this day.

It was a fantastic movie. We sat in the darkness, clutching each other, and trying to figure out who the *Thing* was going to be next. Nothing beats the movies.

After the movies, I had to get over to Brett's and help her with some yard work. Andy and Vinny walked with me because they were going to Pudding Green Hill. Vinny had found an old tire in the woods, and he and Andy were going to roll it down the biggest hill in town.

The day was warm with a slight breeze. I could only see a few thin clouds in the sky. I hoped that Brett would be dressed in shorts when I got to her house. She and my brother lived in the north end of town by the woods. Unfortunately, we had to pass Tim White's house, and it was fast approaching.

Vinny and Andy didn't seem to notice. They were auguring whether or not the *Justice League* had a maid.

"I tell you," Vinny said, kicking a stone on the sidewalk. "There is no way that Wonder Woman and Hawkman clean the bathrooms on their satellite headquarters. They won't even have the time if they wanted to."

Andy shook his head. "You're wrong, chicken legs. They got too many secrets and special equipment up there. They do their own cooking too."

Vinny looked flabbergasted. "Are you mad! Can you see Batman cooking Sunday dinner? Or even Black Canary? She will get her sexy fishnet stockings all dirty."

What a bunch of morons, I thought. They continued to argue as we came up to the White's house. There were no cars in the driveway, and I didn't see the bully out in the yard. Vinny and Andy kept quiet as we began to walk past the house and the tall fenced-in backyard. Somewhere in there was Lucifer, the killer dog of Penny's Creek.

"I do hope he can't jump fences," Vinny stated as his eyes darted around the fence for any signs of the Doberman pinscher.

"Nah," Andy assured him. "I doubt he—" Andy never got to finish because the wooden gate opened, and Tim stepped out.

He looked just as surprised as we were as we stood staring at him. Then, he smiled and ran his hands through his short hair. "Hey, Lucifer, lunch is here. Sic them."

I took one look at Andy; Vinny had already begun to run. We thought the same thing. We were about to die. At the first sound of Lucifer's bark, we took off like sixty down the street behind Vinny.

Andy and I were pretty fast so we caught up to Vinny. I looked back over at my shoulder and saw the Doberman racing down the street after us. I could actually see foam in his mouth. He was big and was definitely what I imagined what he would look like.

"Run faster!" Andy said, slapping me.

I picked up speed and saw Vinny suddenly turn in a yard and start toward a stone wall. I prayed that the dog wouldn't go after him. Lucifer answered my prayers and continued after Andy and I. Andy thought Vinny had a good plan, so he headed for the stone wall too.

Lucifer was gaining fast as I followed Andy. My lungs were screaming for air, and my legs were saying to stop. But I kept running. Andy somehow gained more speed than I and leaped over the wall. Vinny seemed to be hurt as he dragged himself over the wall too. Lucifer barked even louder, and that was when my foot found the small hole in the yard. I went down and fell on my stomach.

I heard Lucifer tearing through the lawn, ready to do serious damage to me. I began to cry and I yelled out loud. "Please. Please don't bite me!" I yelled shutting my eyes.

Then Lucifer began to lick my face, long licks on my neck and up to my eyes, taking the tears from me. I sat up in disbelief. My heart still raced, but I had begun to calm down. I wasn't going to die.

I heard Vinny and Andy climbing back over the wall. Vinny's legs were bleeding where he rammed them into the rock wall. Andy had a huge grin on his face. "Holy crap. Tim's dog is gay!" He started to laugh along with Vinny.

Lucifer barked and began to jump around us. I began to laugh until Andy pointed at me and said "Please, please don't eat me, Mr. Doggy." He began to roll around on the grass with tears rolling down his face.

Oh man, I thought to myself. *I'm never going to leave this down.*

But I was thankful that Lucifer was an angel.

"What a Sally that dog is," Andy said, standing back up and brushing off his grassy blue jeans. He then helped me to my feet.

"No kidding," I said. My heart was still racing like crazy, but I was able to breathe normally again. I looked over at Vinny. He wasn't bleeding too bad but definitely needed Band-Aids or something.

Lucifer wagged his tail and ran around us. I couldn't believe that the town bully had such a nice dog. All this time, we truly thought he was the dog of Satan. Suddenly, I heard someone whistle and Lucifer took off back up the street.

We decided to all go over to Brett's house. There, she could fix Vinny's legs up. I could tell Vinny was in pain, but he wouldn't admit it. Vinny was one tough dude.

Brett was on her front porch, drinking a Budweiser, and writing in a notebook, probably another great story. She was dressed in a yellow sundress and had her long blond hair in pig tails.

"Hey, boys, what's going on?" she asked, waving.

I wanted to say please break up with my brother and marry me. Instead, I told Vinny was in need of some medical supplies. She got off her wicker chair, putting her notebook down. "Vinny! What happened?"

"Lucifer," all three of us said together.

After we told her what happened, she brought us inside where she brought Vinny into the bathroom to patch him up. Andy and I sat in the living room, watching a *James Bond* movie on cable. I had to say this to my brother, Tom. Not only had he had fantastic taste in women, but he also kept up with the times.

I sure didn't have cable at home, same with Andy and Sara. I thought it was the coolest invention ever. Imagine you can watch a full-length movie with no commercials during the day on TV. Tom made good money, and I hoped I would have money like his someday. All I had was $4.07, half of it I found in the couch cushions.

But I was at Brett's house to help out and make the $40 promised by my brother. I would have done it for nothing to help out Brett, but I sure wasn't going to tell him that. Sure, I loved my brother, but he was a jerk to me, so why not.

Vinny and Andy took off after betting to see how long the tire would travel down Pudding Green Hill. I mowed the backyard while Brett did some trimming along her hedges. Afterward, she shared a beer with me on the front porch. It was about 4:30 p.m. now, and I was thinking about what Mom was cooking for dinner.

"Hey, by the way," Brett said, giving me a swat on my head. "I forget to tell you last week when you were here. There are three rules in life, my friend, for all men," she said, showing three fingers.

They were beautiful fingers, I thought.

She had her nails painted light blue. "Number one rule is never ever hit a girl."

I nodded, wondering where she was going with this. "Of course," I said. "I would never."

She nodded in agreement and took another sip of beer. "Number two, never ever rat out your friends. And the third rule in life is always put the damn toilet seat down."

I just stared at her.

"Yeah, put it down there, bud. My fanny got all wet when you crashed over here last week. And I know Tom didn't do it 'cause he knows I'd kick his ass."

I laughed. "I promise."

"Now that we got that out of the way," she said, stretching out her long legs. "What are your and Sara's plans for your birthday?"

Sara and I, strangely, were born on the same day. Actually, we were the only babies born at St Vincent's Hospital on the morning of May 25, 1968. Since we were four where we met in preschool, we've been celebrating our birthdays together.

"Not much. Sheriff Foster is going to barbecue, and we'll probably go see a movie that night."

"How about I take you tubing on the Farmington River?" she suggested.

"You serious?" I asked, jumping out of my chair and almost knocking it down the porch steps.

Brett laughed. "Sure. Invite Heckle and Jekyll too."

Heckle and Jekyll is what Brett called Vinny and Andy sometimes because they were good friends but argued over the dumbest stuff.

"It's a two-hour ride down the river itself," Brett said. "So say, let's leave here about nine thirty in the morning."

I ran over and hugged my sister-in-law. "Thank you, Brett."

She hugged me back.

Chapter 5

B Y MONDAY MORNING, ANDY, Vinny, and Sara had all said they could go. I even invited Parley Whitmore. Parley's father was the first selectman and one of the richest men in town. He usually brought Parley tons of stuff. Parley loved food more than anything, and that was why he was fat. He was no Fat Willy, but he was usually the last picked for gym class. He was a fun guy though.

He was average height for a kid and had curly brown hair. Even curlier than mine. Parley wore usually only two white T-shirts. One had the beautiful Catherine Bach, aka Daisy Duke, on it and the other, the adorable Valerie Bertinelli. His eyesight sucked, so he wore these thick glasses.

"You must thank your sister-in-law for me," he said as we sat in history class, waiting for it to begin.

"You can thank her Saturday morning. You can swim, can't you?"

He shrugged. "I'm no Aquaman, but I won't drown."

I saw Kate Sheppard enter the classroom and sit two rows back from me. She saw me looking at her and smiled. "Hey, Morgan."

I smiled back, knowing my day had gotten even way bigger.

By two that day, the whole school knew that Tim's dog wasn't some demon hellhound, thanks to Andy and his big mouth. I saw him running to different groups of kids during the day, spreading the news. The jerk also made sure everyone knew that I begged the dog not to eat me. I kept expecting Tim to kick his butt, but I didn't see him all day.

Trouble caught up with us on Wednesday though. Andy and I had just walked out of the backdoor at recess when we saw that Fat Willy and Lucas had Sara up against a teacher's station wagon. Jessica Finch, Sara's best female friend, was a few feet away from them, shouting at them to leave Sara alone. Jessica was the shortest girl in our class and had short blond hair. She was nicknamed Tinkerbelle.

Without even talking to each other, Andy and I both walked over to them. "Leave her alone, Grimus," Andy said to Willy.

The bully turned, glaring at Andy. His purple T-shirt had numerous mustard spots from lunch. As I said before, Willy didn't believe in napkins or any fashion statements. "Well, well, if it is short stuff and jerk head."

"You okay?" I asked Sara. I was scared. I never confronted the bullies before, and I knew Andy couldn't take both of them in a fight.

She nodded. But I knew she was scared, and I saw tears in her eyes.

"I hear you are spreading rumors about Tim," Lucas said folding his arms. He spat on the ground.

"Rumors my butt," Andy said. "Just telling the truth."

Jessica laughed but quickly shut up when Willy glared at her. "Shut up, Tinkerbelle."

Lucas laughed, slapping Willy on his back. "We heard that Morgan crapped his pants when Lucifer was chasing him."

I expected Andy to laugh again, but he just shook his head. "We all know the truth."

Fat Willy walked over and got into his face. Immediately, I saw fear creep into Andy's eyes. "You are getting a lot of balls there, Donahue, but you best back off." Andy took a step back.

I looked around and saw a few other kids watching us. Ms. Lamb was trying to organize a kickball game with the fourth graders, but I could tell she was looking over at us.

"Get lost, tubs," Sara said, walking back over to Jessica.

"Just because you are the sheriff's kid doesn't make you safe from Tim and us," Willy said, smiling. His eyes roamed up and down over Jessica's trim body. "You might go missing too."

Andy actually let out a roar and tried to punch Willy. The fat boy took a step back, avoiding the punch. I saw Ms. Lamb hurrying over to us. I sure didn't want us getting detentions for fighting, so I tried to hold Andy back.

Andy was furious. He raced toward Willy again, but somehow, I managed to hold onto him. "You can tell Tim if he wants to start a war with me and my friends, then do it already!" Andy shouted. "Until then, you leave her and my friends alone!"

Lucas and Willy laughed and then quickly hurried away as Ms. Lamb approached.

"What on earth is going on here?" she demanded. Ms. Lamb taught us English and was our favorite teacher, but she was strict.

Andy broke out of my grasp and walked off, with Jessica chasing after him.

"Well, Morgan?" the teacher asked.

"Nothing, Ms. Lamb," I said. "Just messing around."

"Nothing to worry about," Sara said, throwing her arm around my shoulder. "We were just arguing who the best baseball team was."

Ms. Lamb nodded, but she knew Sara was full of it. She walked back over to the disorganized kickball game. Sara and I raced over to Andy, who sat down near the seesaw. Jessica was whispering to him. Everyone knew that she liked Andy.

"That was something," I said to him, squatting down next to him. "You sounded just like Wyatt Earp or something."

Andy grinned, but I knew he was still fuming inside. I never saw him so upset. Not even the time when his father grounded him for two weeks for shooting frogs with his BB gun.

"You know fatso is going to tell Tim what he said," Sara said to us. She picked up a small stone and threw it across the grass.

"Let him," I told her. I was getting sick and tired of those guys, especially now that they messed with Sara. But I knew we were all in deep trouble.

I got to Brett's at eight forty-five Saturday morning with Parley and Vinny. It was a little cool, but the weatherman said it was going to be a warm and sunny day. We were dressed in our bathing suits and had a change of clothing in our backpacks, along with a towel each. Brett met us at the porch steps, and she was carrying a picnic basket. "Morning, everyone," she said cheerfully.

We couldn't respond. We just stared at Brett. She was wearing a hot pink bikini with pink sandals. I'm not sure if I told you but she was almost a twin of Cheryl Ladd. She gave me a kiss on my cheek and wished me a happy birthday. She walked over to her pickup truck and put the basket in the back.

"Hummina, hummina—" Vinny said, with his mouth open.

"Um, oh," he paused, thinking for a moment. "What's the last one?"

"Hummina," Parley told him, shaking his head.

I couldn't blame my friend though for forgetting. She was like a Greek goddess. Well, an Irish goddess anyway. We heard a horn honk, and Tika's red Jeep pulled up with Andy and Sara. "Let's go rolling, you punk asses," Tika yelled out the window. "The river is waiting."

Sara and I rode with Brett in her truck while the boys rode in Tika's Wrangler, each of them drooling at the redhead in her green bikini. The windows were down, and "Kiss" was playing on the radio as we drove through town, heading for the highway.

As I said before, Penny's Creek was a small town. Sidewalks lined most of the streets, and the town kept the many oak, evergreen, and maple trees and shrubs trimmed beautifully. Last year, Penny's Creek was number three of the most beautiful towns in Connecticut. The population was mainly Irish and Italian and a few Koreans. The majority were Christians, probably 60 percent were Catholics. It was settled back in 1878 after a small population of Irish immigrants left New York City to form their own town on the banks of the Connecticut River.

Everyone got along for the most part, and crime was nonexistent till the kids started disappearing. The town council vetoed First Selectman Whitmore's idea of installing a curfew. All the kids were taken in daylight hours, and as my dad told me, the town didn't want to give any more power to Parley's dad. The man was power-hungry, according to him.

Sheriff Foster was in the process of hiring two more officers, and additional patrols were now seen hourly up and down the streets. Among them were Tika's ex-boyfriend, Clinton Rushmore, the sheriff's number one man. I personally thought Clinton was a dick because he dumped Tika. Only a big horse's ass or an insane lunatic would break up with her.

Parents were warned to have their children not walk alone and use a buddy system with friends. No one was allowed to walk home from school by themselves.

Brett, Sara, and I talked about school, the Yankee's, Brett's newest story, and how Mrs. Hewitt at Nelson's Grocery store was the worst bagger alive. We arrived at the Farmington River by 10:15 a.m. Sara and I had gone there once before with Brett and Tom, but as for the others, this was their first time, and they were super excited.

We paid for our big yellow or orange tubes and were told to put on our life vests, which we promptly took off once in the water. We made our way down the path, swearing as we stepped on small stones or twigs, wishing someone would invent some kind of water shoe. We each got on onto our tubes and pushed off and died in laughter watching Parley attempting to adjust his large body on the yellow tube. He refused to take off his Daisy Duke shirt as well.

The width of the river, at some points, was at least sixty feet across. The water was clean and cool. Not cold. It felt like drinking a cool glass of water on a warm day, except you were in the glass instead.

Luckily, the cool water helped Parley, Andy, Vinny, and I keep our male hood in hibernation as we tried not to stare at Brett and Tika's hotness. Sara looked great too. She was definitely mature for her age. Not a body like Kate Sheppard but she was going to break a lot of hearts.

There were at least a few hundred people on the river that morning. The seven of us tried to stay together as much as we could, but there were rapids that separated us a few times. Parley spent most of his time getting stuck on the river edge. Andy was doing his best to talk to a high schoolgirl while Vinny got off his tube and swam for a while.

I found myself next to my fellow birthday girl. She had her eyes closed as the sun warmed her face, and her hand trailed in the water. Her brown hair was in pigtails. It was quiet on the river with the occasional laughter from the other tubers.

"What are Andy's chances with that high school chick?" I asked her.

She looked over and smiled. "About a thousand to one."

After a few moments, she spoke again. "You never said if the dream catcher worked?" she asked me.

I felt bad that I hadn't said anything to her. "So far, she has stayed away," I said.

"I know you don't like talking about her," Sara said, gently looking over at me, "but I want to make sure you are okay."

I didn't hide anything from Sara, and she knew it. "I'll let you know if she comes back."

She nodded and then splashed me. "If she does, I'm going to kick her wrinkled butt."

It was a great birthday present my sister-in-law gave me. Two long hours in the outdoors on a cool, long river with my best friends in the world.

Chapter 6

AT 4:00 P.M., THERE was a cookout at the Foster's where my parents, Brett, Tika, and I went to. Sheriff Foster and my dad drank beers and made bad jokes as they grilled hamburgers, barbecue chicken, and hot dogs. My mom, Mrs. Foster, Tika, and Brett sat at the picnic table, drinking wine and gossiping about the latest Penny's Creek news. I tossed the Frisbee around with Sara and her little sister, Christy.

Dinner was delicious especially with Mrs. Foster's famous potato salad and Tika's warm brownies. My parents gave me the Adventure game for Atari, the new Stepen King Book *"Different Seasons"* and a Notre Dame Sweatshirt. Sara got a new tape player and some clothes.

At six, Sara and I walked downtown to meet up with Andy, Vinny, and Jessica Finch to see *Poltergeist*. We stuck to the sidewalks and kept watching for anyone suspicious, like we promised our parents. We were discussing what sports or clubs we would join this fall in high school.

"I just don't see you as a cheerleader," I said to her.

"Oh," she grunted as she jumped over someone's dropped vanilla ice-cream cone on the sidewalk. "You see me as a football player instead?"

"Well, you are always kicking our butts. Don't take this the wrong way, but you aren't a girly girl 24/7. Cheerleaders are. They don't play whiffle ball and play in the creek." They like to sit around talking about movie stars and JR on *Dallas*.

Sara did her eye-rolling thing. "How is it that you are an expert on the most useless shit and haven't really ever kissed a girl?"

"I have so," I protested and then quickly shut my mouth. I pretended to be interested in a gray squirrel that just run up a maple tree near us. I knew my face was red.

"That was a stupid dare from Andy." Sara laughed slapping my back. "And it was me on the receiving end."

She laughed for a few more seconds as we neared Trumbull Street. "Seriously, just man up and ask her out. Go to the movies or the café. Tika or Brett will drive you, so you won't feel like sap if your parents drove instead."

"Maybe," I muttered, bending down to tie my shoe. I wondered if I could get up the nerve to ask Kate out. I mean I could always go up to a girl and talk to her, but to actually let them know I like them and ask her out, heck no!

"Hurry up, Morg," Sara said, stepping off the curb. "We're going to be late."

That was when the red van came peeling around the corner and struck her.

Sara's funeral was on Wednesday morning. A good portion of Penny's Creek attended. I found myself sitting in between my mother and Brett while Father Daniels delivered what should have been an uplifting eulogy, but I just felt worse and stared at the closed coffin. Tom had come back from his business trip and stood at the other side of my mom. Tom was not an emotional man, but I saw tears in his eyes too.

The doctor Smiths said Sara died almost instantly. They assured me, and others, that she probably never felt a thing. I guess that was the only blessing I could find in it. The driver of the red van never stopped, and there was no trace of it in town.

Brett squeezed my hand, but I barely noticed. I hadn't spoken a word after Officer Clinton questioned me on Friday, after the accident. All I remembered was running out to the street and seeing blood all over. I cradled Sara in my arms and screamed for someone to help me.

Someone, eventually, gently took her out of my arms. I remember Sheriff Foster arriving on the scene and crying out his daughter's name. Either Clinton or Officer Duva had to hold him back.

I saw Vinny sitting a few pews behind me with his mom, who gently smiled at me. Andy and Parley sat with their parents on the other side. Jessica Finch as MIA, and Andy never looked up once. Tika sat on the other side of Brett, holding onto Christy who seemed to be the only one who was aware that Sara was truly gone. Sara was buried under a tall oak tree at the Resurrection Cemetery. Her engraving read, "Beloved daughter, sister, and friend. Soar high."

On the night Sara was buried, I woke up and took a sip of water out of the glass beside my bed. My bedroom was dark except for the light from the street. I lay back down and heard a rattling noise from across the room. I sat up and saw the closet door was open. A long chain dangled from a hanger and was swinging back and forth. Then, I heard her breathing. She was in the corner of the room, up on the ceiling. The old woman's fingernails had dug into the ceiling like a dog's paws would make on snow. Hazel laughed and quickly crawled across the ceiling toward me.

I woke up screaming and said the only three more words that week after my parents rushed in to comfort me. "She is back," I said.

Chapter 7

I DIDN'T ATTEND SCHOOL THAT Thursday and Friday. I was sure I was behind everyone else with one whole week of missed school. But I didn't care. Homework, dodgeball, lunch, who discovered the West Indies, 7×9=, what is a common word? I mean who really gives a shit when it comes down to it. Sara was dead, and she was never coming back.

My parents left me alone for the most part. They didn't make me go to school or ask how I was feeling. They knew how. When you think about it, that is a dumb thing to say to a person after they lose someone close to them. How do you feel, or how are you doing? Just as stupid as asking someone who just hit themselves with a hammer and they are bleeding and swearing up a storm if they were alright.

Now, I didn't become some hermit that hid in his room the whole day. I read my comics and *Choose Your Own Adventure* novels, I rode my bike up and down my street, and I still ate with my parents and Brett and Tom, who had come over for dinner each night that week. I played Checkers with Tom, cards with my dad, and Asteroids with Brett. I just didn't talk. I couldn't, even if I wanted to. I slept pretty well and only dreamt of Hazel once more that week.

Sunday afternoon, Sara's mother rang our doorbell. I was in my room, staring at the fish in my new fish tank my dad got me the day before. It was a ten-gallon tank with five tropical fish in it. One of them was an iridescent shark that I named Jaws. I could just sit and stare at the fish for hours. They were amazing to watch. Green and yellow plants rose up from the small light blue stones at the bottom of the tank. Jaws chased the fat orange fish around the plants. I kept hoping that Jaws would go crazy and start to eat the other fish, but so far, nothing like that happened.

My mother knocked at my door. "Honey, Mrs. Foster is downstairs. She wants to see you for a minute."

I nodded and followed her downstairs. Mrs. Foster had chosen to wait outside on the front porch. It was a sunny day, and she greeted me warmly and gave me a hug. I thought she was going to look horrible, but her hair was down in a long braid and her yellow spring dress looked new.

"I know you aren't talking much these days," she said gently as she sat next to me on the wooden porch chairs. "So I won't trouble you for long. I just wanted to give you these."

I noticed she was holding a large brown shopping bag. She pressed her lips together and handed me the bag. I looked at her puzzled.

"She would have wanted you to have these," Sara's mom said. She blinked back some tears. "It's not much. Just her Yankee hat, a few records, and some pictures of you guys."

I nodded and took the bag. I didn't know what to do.

Mrs. Foster stood up so I followed. She gave me a long hug and patted my back. "She would have done anything or gone anywhere with you, Morgan," Mrs. Foster whispered. "She loved you so."

And then, she quickly retreated down the steps and headed toward her station wagon. Just before she got to it, she turned and waved at me. "Come see Christy when you can. She would love to see you."

Then, Sara's mom got into her car and drove away. I sat outside for another half hour, just staring at the bag.

Brett and Tom had just left shortly after dinner when Vinny walked into my room. I was reading a *Flash* comic, lying on my bed. "What's up, you Irish bastard?" he asked, plopping himself down onto my red bean bag. He was eating a green apple, most likely offered by my mother.

I looked over at him, shrugged, and kept reading.

Vinny was quiet for a few seconds, which had to be hard for the yapper he was. He looked over at my fish tank and whistled. "Cool fish. I like this fat orange one. "You should name him Tang." Vinny drank that stuff like three times a day. So are you coming back to school tomorrow? We got a history quiz on the Boston Tea Party."

I shrugged and kept reading.

"Will you put that down, damn it, and talk to me!" Vinny shouted, jumping up from the bean bag.

I put the comic book down and opened my mouth to speak, but I felt the tears coming so I shut my mouth again.

Vinny swore and walked over to my new fish tank and tapped on it. "Tinkerbelle doesn't talk anymore either," he said. "She ran from English class yesterday, crying. Andy can't even get her to smile."

I wanted to tell him that Jessica Finch was always emotional but kept silent. I didn't know how Jessica was really feeling. After all, she was Sara's best female friend.

"Andy and Tika say hey, Artie too. He has last week's comics on hold for you."

I lay back down on my bed and stared at the *Charlie's Angels* poster on my ceiling. The beautiful Cheryl Ladd stared down back at me.

"Well, I guess I'll see you around," Vinny said, walking toward my bedroom door. He paused for a moment and look back at me. "She was my friend too, asshole." He slammed the door shut.

Tuesday afternoon, I found myself at the section of Penny's Creek that ran behind Sara's house. We sometimes would come down there and hang out. It was our secret hideout. We had a secret stash of soda and candy bars kept in plastic bags under some rocks. We even had three cans of beer and a May 1980 issue of Playboy that Andy had swiped from one of his brothers.

I sat on my favorite large rock and listened as the water trickled over the small stones and a blue jay sang in a tall pine tree above me. The day was cloudy but warm, and summer was just about here.

Shortly after, Haywire stepped out of the woods and stood beside the creek about fifteen feet away from me. As I said before, Haywire was the town crazy and was harmless. At least, I have heard he was. The man was dressed in brown pants with a tear running down the seam of the left leg. He had on a gray Chewbacca T-shirt, and his gray hair stood wildly up but seemed clean. He wore his usual black boots.

"Hello," he said simply.

I nodded and looked around me, hoping to find another person. I had never been this close to the crazy before, and I wasn't sure how to handle it.

"Your friend was always nice to me," he said, still staring down into the creek.

Sara talked to him? She must have been braver than I thought. She had never mentioned it to me before.

"She knew about them too," Haywire said. "She asked me about them." He brushed a fly out of his face and then, turned toward me. "Beware, Morgan. They are in there."

Now, Haywire always talked crazy, and this afternoon was no exception. But since he was talking about Sara, I was interested. But then, he quickly turned away, almost stumbling into the creek. "The woods has them!" he shouted and walked off. I heard him running through the woods, stepping on several tree branches.

"What was his deal?" a familiar female voice asked.

I looked up to find the beautiful Tika Murphy standing next to me. I never even heard her approach but could guess that was why Haywire suddenly ran off.

"What did he want?" she asked sitting down beside me.

I was happy to see Tika. She looked beautiful in the woods. She was wearing tans shorts and white Converse All Stars. She had on a green blouse that gave me an ample amount of cleavage to stare at it.

I just shook my head.

"I hear you have said barely seven words since the accident." She looked over at me and ran her hand through my hair. "At least you are showering," she smiled.

I returned the smile. I couldn't help it. The redhead just had one of those contagious smiles.

"Vinny tells me you haven't been in school for over a week now. He is very worried about you. We all are," she said, putting her arm around my shoulders. She smelt great.

I opened my mouth but once again closed it.

"I know how you feel, my friend," she said.

I grimaced that phrase I hated. That was another thing I hated. People always saying how they know how once feels. I loved Tika, but now, she was getting me mad.

"I'm still not over my sister's death. I guess I never will," Tika said, and I felt her tense up. I remembered she had lost her sister a few years ago. Maybe she really did know how I felt.

"When she died, I just wanted to hide away from the world. But that's really impossible when others are in your face asking how you are or what they can do for you. So I chose to keep silent. Felt if I didn't talk that, the onslaught of cries wouldn't come pouring out of me. I knew I would just cry and cry and cry and then, probably cry some more. I wanted to stay strong for some dumb reason, but then, I couldn't take it anymore. So one day, when I was at work, I broke down. It actually felt pretty good to get it all out."

I was shocked. Tika knew exactly what I was feeling.

A tear rang down Tika's face. She was quiet for a few moments, and she picked up a small stone and threw it into the water. Then, she spoke again. "Then, I moved here because Artie asked me to, and I met Brett who became like another sister to me. You got the greatest sister-in-law there, Morg. And then little Sara Foster. Little sis," she paused for a moment and stared up at the trees as if she was trying to get her emotions in check. "That girl, well, you don't find too many like her. I'm going to miss her so damn much."

I nodded my head but still said nothing.

"So you missing all this school and ignoring your friends is not good, Morgan. If you continue to do this all summer, it's not good at all. It's unfair to your parents and brother, it's unfair to Vinny and Andy, and unfair to Brett and I." She turned my head toward hers. "And it's unfair to Sara. She wouldn't want you to keep doing this. Nothing good can come from it."

She waited a few seconds, expecting me to cry or say something. But that didn't happen. She patted my thigh, and she stood up. "If you want to talk, or just not be alone, you know where to find me," she said and began to walk off.

"Tika," I barely got out.

She stopped and turned surprised. "Yeah?"

"Will you buy me an ice cream cone?" I asked, smiling.

She laughed, and her laughter felt so good to hear. "Two scoops."

That was when I got up from my favorite rock and ran over to her and let those tears finally come to pass. And Tika was right. It felt good.

Chapter 8

TUESDAY MORNING, I RETURNED to school. Nothing much seemed to change. Kids were talking about the Yankees-Tigers game from the night before, a skinny sixth grader walked down the hall, unaware he had a kick me sign on his back; and one of the toilets in the girls' bathroom had backed up.

I walked over to Vinny's locker, where he was unpacking his backpack. "Hey, you Italian bastard," I said.

He looked up at me and shook his head. "Glad to see the cat didn't really get your tongue."

"Yea," I replied. "You don't seem too surprised to see me here."

"I'm not," he said, hanging up his backpack onto one of the hooks inside his locker. "After all, who doesn't cheer up from a visit from the Irish Goddess?"

I smiled. "Very true, my friend."

He closed his locker, almost dropping his American history book.

"Sorry," I said to him. "I just couldn't deal."

"It's cool. Guess we will all miss Sara in our own way. Come on, we got that quiz now. I'll let you copy my answers."

I laughed as we walked down the hall. "Copy your answers? I don't want to fail," I said. I saw Kate Sheppard down at the other end, and she gave me a quick wave before going into her class.

You going to ask her out or not? That was one of the last things Sara had said to me, and I decided I need to do it very soon.

After history class, where I pretty much bombed but wasn't going to lose sleep over it, I had English. I met up with Andy in front of the classroom door and was surprised to see him holding hands with Tinkerbelle.

"Welcome back," Andy said, slapping me a high five.

Jessica stared at me for a few seconds, and I noticed she was staring at the Yankee hat I had on. The short blond hair girl always seemed to study someone or something before speaking, as if she was thinking of what to say. "Her hat looks good on you." she smiled.

I shrugged, afraid I was about to cry, when I heard someone breathing heavily behind me. I turned to see Fat Willy and Tim White standing there.

Fat Willy was wearing this bright orange sweatpants that seemed to contain stains from every major food group.

"Hey, fancy pants," Andy said, grinning.

Even Tim laughed at that for a few seconds. He was dressed in a jean jacket with a peace sign on the collar. "Morgan," he stated staring down at me.

As I said before, Tim was a tall dude, but then again, everyone was taller than me. I held my ground and stared back at the bully.

"Watch your mouth, Donahue," Fat Willy said to my friend. "Or I'll pound your short pal here."

I tensed, thinking I was about to be hit by the fat jerk.

"Back off, Will," Tim told him.

"Sorry about Sara," he said, looking down at the floor as if he was studying his shoes. "She was pretty cool."

What the hell? I looked over at Andy and Jessica who seemed just as shocked as I was. The colossal jerk actually sounded sincere.

"My friends won't mess with you guys for the rest of the week," Tim said, looking back up at me. "Give you time to get over her."

But then, he glared at Andy and rubbed the scar on his face. "But this Sunday, we fight."

Then Willy and Tim walked down the hall. "Can we make it Saturday?" Andy yelled after them. "I got company coming on Sunday!"

Fat Willy answered with the middle finger.

Andy laughed and looked at the worry on my face. "As I said, Morgan, welcome back."

Wednesday night I had dinner over at Vinny's, and Mrs. Catalano cooked up a delicious pot roast, roasted potatoes, and carrots. We quickly did our homework before watching *Three's Company*. Vinny was a Chrissie/Suzanne Summers fan, but I preferred Cindy/Jenilee Harrison. Best legs on TV.

When I got home, I heard my dad talking on the phone about how neither the owner nor the red van, that had killed Sara, had been found. The sheriff's men were up to their eyeballs, looking for the four missing kids. Sheriff Foster was on his own quest to find who killed his daughter.

Mayor Whitmore, unable to instill a curfew, hired two more men on the Penny's Creek force. Plus, over a hundred volunteers had formed under the mayor's direction to scour the woods around town. Parley's dad was a power-hungry jerk, but the man sure could run a town I always thought.

Friday was a half day, so Vinny, Andy, and I were going to meet downtown to sign up for the young police recruits. But first, I stopped by Tim White's house, and after watching for a while and seeing Tim wasn't home, I walked up to the fenced-in yard.

I heard Lucifer moving around, and I slipped two hotdogs through a crack in the wood. I heard the Doberman wolf them down. "Good boy," I said and walked off. I had been by to see Tim's dog about four times, ever since he chose not to eat me. I knew Tim was mean to his dog, and I thought I'd give him some extra love. I had always wanted a dog.

About fifteen kids had shown up at the park. Officer Clinton Rushmore was sitting behind a folded-out table, with pamphlets and booklets spread out before him.

"I didn't know this butthead was going to be in charge," Vinny muttered. My skinny friend did not care for Clinton. Not because he was strong, powerful, and good-looking with sandy-blond hair, but the way he treated Tika. He hurt her pretty bad when they broke up, and Artie had told us that she cried for weeks.

Clinton was a jerk, I had to admit, but he was one of the sheriff's most trusted officers, and I figured I could learn a lot from him.

"Step up here, boys, and learn all about the town's first young recruits," the officer said. "You will be taught in the fine points of martial arts, safety, and communication as well as be given your own whistle."

Andy chuckled. "Oh, did you hear that, men? A whistle!"

I grinned but continued to listen.

"You will be given certain hours, where you can help patrol our streets with our officers, making this town the safest town in Connecticut. So sign up."

A tall Oriental woman, about twenty-five, walked up behind Clinton and gave him a long kiss on the lips. A few kids whistled.

"Excuse me, Officer Clinton, where do I sign up for that!" Vinny asked. The kids standing around him and broke into laughter.

Clinton gave him a glare and then whispered to his new girlfriend. She smiled and walked away. The boys and two girls lined up and began to fill out the forms on the table.

"Uh, why are we doing this stupid thing again?" Andy asked as he put Vinny into a headlock. My friend struggled to get out.

"Something new to do," I answered him.

He and Vinny continued to wrestle with each other, with Andy clearly winning. As I said before, Andy loved to push us around at times. Vinny said the reason why was because Andy had gotten his ass kicked in so many times by his three older brothers, so it was the time Andy dished it out to the both of us.

The line moved quickly, and I found myself signing up for a first aid class next week and also a ride along with Officer Duva. Not much happened in Penny's Creek but I hoped that maybe someone would rob the bank or a brawl would break out at the bar.

We decided to stop at the comic book shop, where Vinny professed his love for Tika, and Artie traded out insults with Andy and I about our heritage. It was a pretty good afternoon until Parley Whitmore came running into the CCC and told us that Haywire had been arrested on the charges of kidnapping.

That night, my mother and father had an argument at dinner about Haywire. My mom believed the man was crazy and probably hurt the missing children. But then again, my mother thought that most people were crazy. My dad argued, though Haywire was the town crazy, he really has never caused trouble. It was just First Selectman Whitmore trying to show that he is doing something about the situation.

Ever since the third kid had gone missing, news channels from all over the country had dropped in on our little town, breaking the story about the missing children. It wasn't every day kids disappeared from their own yards and streets. Even the state police helped search the nearby woods and streets of Penny's Creek. But as weeks went by, less and less news people came, and it had been over two weeks since a kid had gone missing.

I didn't think Haywire had kidnapped the kids. Why would he? Plus, when I saw him at the creek in the beginning of the week, he acted like he wanted to tell me something. I just hoped no one else would disappear.

I went to sleep that night after watching a rerun of *What's Happening*. I didn't dream about Hazel nor did I dream about Sara. The next morning, my parents had gone off to their weekend boring errands, and I decided to head into town to see if there was any news regarding Haywire. I called Parley to come with me, hoping he would have some info since he was the mayor's kid.

We ate a couple of green apples as we headed into town. It was a warm day, and we both were dressed in shorts and T-shirts, with Parley wearing his trademark Valerie Bertinelli shirt. Parley had heard his dad talking with a few officers at his house last night, and they were going to let Haywire go. They had no real proof that Haywire had done anything, and it was just Office Clinton that had arrested him on some stupid suspicion. As I said before, Clinton was a jerk and was always breaking someone's balls. Guess this week, it was Haywire's turn.

Outside kids were riding their bikes, playing kickball, and we even saw a few playing ding-dong ditch. Lawns were being cut, and we stopped to watch a cute high schoolgirl washing her red Volkswagen. It was a typical Saturday morning.

As we neared Main Street, we saw Vinny riding his bike toward us, waving his hands frantically. "What's up with Skinny Vinny?" Parley asked.

I shrugged and waited for Vinny to ride up to us. He was wearing his army camouflage pants. His face was red, and he was sweating. "Big trouble man. Like big time."

"What trouble?" I asked him as I chucked my apple core into the sewer drain.

"Tim White is what's up," Vinny said, getting off his bike and putting down his kickstand. Vinny had a Huffy that had been run over by a pickup truck last fall. Though the bike still worked, it was beat to hell, but Vinny didn't want to give it up even though his mom said she'd buy him another one.

"Tim White is at the vacant lot, talking to a bunch of dudes. Saying he is going to kill us like real bad!"

Parley looked as if he was going to have a heart attack. I was a little scared myself. "Who is he with?"

"His usual crew, Fat Willy and Lucas. Also, Nick the Slick."

Nick the Slick was a ninth grader that hung around Tim sometimes. He got his name because he slicked his hair back with tons of hair oils.

"I'm going home," Paley said, turning around.

I grabbed his arm and told him to hold up. My friends looked at me, hoping that I had some plan. "You see Andy this morning?"

"Probably still sleeping. You know him. He stays up late, hoping to see nudity on cable."

My two friends looked at me, wanting me to make a decision. I nodded. "All right. Let him sleep." I began to walk toward Main Street again.

"Where the hell are you going?" Vinny shouted at me. "We need a plan."

"I'm going to get a Pepsi and a jelly doughnut at the Nelson's," I told him.

Ten minutes later, I was sitting on the curb outside of Nelson's grocery store, eating my breakfast. Parley sat next to me, and for the first time in my life, he refused to eat anything. I knew he was nervous and so was I, but I doubted Tim was really going to kill us. Beat us up maybe, which wouldn't be fun either, but for some reason, I was feeling brave.

A red-haired kid from sixth grade came riding up with a few of his friends. He had this stupid grin on his face. "You are all wanted at the vacant lot by Mr. White."

I burst out laughing. "Mr. White?"

The kid nodded. "He wants to see you and your friends now."

Parley began to stand up. "I'm going to tell my dad."

I jumped up and faced him. "You'll do no such thing. We have to take care of this ourselves." I had no idea what I was thinking at the time.

"But Morgan," he complained. He was shaking so bad I thought his glasses were going to fall off. He opened his mouth to say something else when we saw Vinny and Andy riding up. Vinny still looked as if he had biked over a thousand miles, but Andy looked like he was ready for a fight. Parley pointed at me. "He's gone loco." "He wants to fight Tim."

"I didn't say that," I said. "But I'm getting sick of him picking on us."

Andy spit on the ground. He ran his hands through his crew cut. "Me too. Hate that jerk and that fat tub he hangs out with."

He turned his bike around. "Come on let's do this."

Vinny looked as if he was going to have a heart attack. It wasn't because he was afraid. Skinny Vinny wasn't really scared of much of anything except rejection from girls. But I knew he didn't want us just to go there without some kind of plan.

"If you don't go, you guys are chicken," the sixth grader muttered.

Andy walked over and grabbed his handlebars. "Listen, you red-haired jerk. How about I start beating your ass with your face?"

I wondered what it be like to see one would beat someone with their own face, but the kid shut his mouth immediately and rode away with his friends. Probably heading to tell Tim. My friends looked at me, waiting for me to tell them what to do.

"Come on," I said. I jumped onto the handlebars of Andy's bike, and Parley jumped onto Vinny's beat-up Huffy, and we made our way to the vacant lot by Penny's creek. We didn't know what was going to happen, but we knew we had to show up or we would be branded as chickens for the rest of our lives. And being branded a chicken in Penny's Creek was a death sentence.

"Let's just kick them in the gonads," Vinny suggested.

I had no clue what the four of us were going to do. We had no plan. Just a crazy urge to face our bullies. I really missed Sara right then. She would know what to do. It was then that Sara sent a message in a strange way. Jessica Finch was standing on the street, right before Penny's creek. She was with the lovely Kate Sheppard. Kate had on a yellow blouse and jean shorts. She had her long black hair in a ponytail. She looked gorgeous.

Jessica gave a big smile to Andy as I hopped off his bike. She had a gray backpack on, which I recognized as an old one of Sara's. "Tinkerbelle, what's up?" I asked.

"Heard you boys are in a little bit of trouble," she said.

Andy crossed his arms over each other. "When aren't we?" he grinned.

"You guys really going to fight Tim and his gang?" Kate asked. She had a look of concern. I barely nodded, afraid to say something stupid. "You are pretty brave, Morgan."

"Morgan! What about me!" Vinny complained, almost falling off his bike. "I'm brave as they came."

I heard a couple yell from down the street. It sounded like it came from the vacant lot. I looked over at Kate. "Well, I don't want to fight, but we have to do something."

Tinkerbelle tapped my shoulder. "That's why I'm here."

She took off the gray backpack and bent down on the ground. "Sara had prepared for this."

What was she talking about? I wondered. I bent down next to Jessica as she opened up Sara's backpack. I smiled as I saw what was inside. Leave it to Sara Foster to save the day.

"She told me about this last fall. Pretty sure you guys may need it," Jessica said, looking at the four of us.

"I think Sara just gave us a plan," Vinny said, rubbing his hands together.

Tim White, Fat Willy, Lucas Jackson, and Nick the Slick were standing on a couple of big rocks at the edge of the vacant lot. About twelve kids from school were crowded around them. Tim and Lucas had their shirts off, as if they were waiting for some wrestling match. Thank God, Fat Willy had kept his purple T-shirt on. They seemed to be bragging about what they were going to do to my friends and I.

We stood on the other side of the lot, waiting for them to see us. Jessica and Kate stood in line with us too, with the backpack open on the ground in front of us. "You really should get out of her," I whispered to Kate.

She took my hand and squeezed it. "It's not just you guys who are getting bullied by them. I'm sick of it as well."

I wanted to ask her to marry me right then but was interrupted by Fat Willy yelling and pointing at us. "Look, it's the fantastic dorks!" he shouted.

Andy spit on the ground. "And it's Grimus and his gay friends."

Parley groaned next to me. "And here I was hoping we were going to talk them out of it."

Tim jumped off the rocks, followed by his three friends. "Told you we are going to get it today. You even asked for Saturday to be the day."

My mouth felt like it was filled with cotton balls. "If you leave now, we won't hurt you."

Tim burst out laughing, along with his jerk friends. A couple of the other kids joined in as well. I had to admit it sounded pretty funny too.

Fat Willy started toward us. "I'm going to take you first, Donahue," he said to Andy. "And then, I'm going to take on Tinkerbelle. Have a little fun with that blond if you know what—"

And with that, we let them have it. Last fall, Sara must have spent a lot of time in the woods, collecting our arsenal. She found the best dirt clods, aka dirt bombs, imaginable. They were hard but would break upon impact and definitely would inflict pain. Most were the size of golf balls but some were bigger. The one thrown by Andy hit Fat Willy right in his fat stomach. He let out a wail of pain.

Two dirt clods smashed into Lucas's shoulder, compliments of Kate and Vinny, while Parley threw one at Nick's head. He missed by a mile, but I hit him right where it counted, twice!

Nick the Slick fell to knees, crying for us to stop. That he would never hurt us, forgetting the time he stole my sneakers on my way home from school once. Serves him right as I threw another dirt bomb.

Tim had crossed the vacant lot, avoiding the bombardment. He bore down on us like a locomotive, but we all aimed for him pretty much at the same time. He was hit five times with the dirt clods, and he fell down, covering his head. He shouted for us to stop.

Fat Willy was crying, and Nick was still rolling around, clutching his crotch. Lucas was bleeding from the forehead and looked confused. All the other kids were shouting for us, and then, a few of them began to throw a few dirt bombs themselves.

Fat Willy ran off, followed by Lucas. I let one more dirt clod go, and it smashed right onto the back of the retreating fat bully.

We stopped throwing the dirt bombs and stared at Tim lying on the ground. He wasn't bleeding, but I could see he was hurting. And most of it was his pride. Noticing that we had stopped our attack, he got to his feet and opened his mouth.

"Get lost," Andy growled, ready to throw another.

He glared at him and then actually ran off as well. Nick the Slick took after him, yelling at him to wait up. And that was how the dirt bomb fight of '82 happened.

Chapter 9

$\mathcal{I}$ WOKE UP THAT NIGHT because I felt as if someone was watching me sleep. My bedroom was pitch black, and I could hear a thunderstorm going through town. The rain was coming down hard, and I could hear it hitting my window.

"Dad," I asked, thinking he was in my room, but I didn't get an answer. I turned over on my side to face the window when the lightning flash. The room lit up, showing the old woman lying next to me in bed inches away from me.

She smiled, showing her six yellow teeth.

I should have screamed or even hit her, but I froze.

Hazel spoke in a soft whisper. "Do you think when you die you go to heaven?" A trickle of blood ran out of her nose. She smiled. "You come to me."

I woke up screaming, barely noticing my mother hugging me.

The next morning during breakfast, my mother lay a plate of scrambled eggs down. "Your father has to go to Tulsa on business on Tuesday for two weeks. I thought of going with him, but I'm not so sure now."

I looked up at her. Geesh, two weeks without my parents would be awesome. What else was there in life? "Why not?" I asked her.

"Your nightmares, honey. They are getting worse."

I shrugged but she was right. Since Sara died, Hazel had been coming to torment me most nights now. The dream catcher that Sara gave me was now under my bed. It hurt me too much to look at it. But there wasn't jack squat my parents could do anyways.

"I'll be okay. I can take care of myself."

My mother laughed and rubbed my hair. "Yeah, like I would leave you home alone for that long. I was going to have Brett watch you since Tom is in France."

Yeah, I thought. Brett sure was going to think I'm really the one for her if she needs to watch me. But then, I thought Brett was great, and spending two weeks with her would be a dream come true. Plus, I was planning to ask Kate out for this Friday, and Brett driving us on the date would be way better than my mom.

"Brett can handle me just fine, Mom. Seriously, I'm going to high school next year."

She watched me for a few moments as I ate my eggs. "All right, then. I'll go with Dad, and Brett can stay here or you with her."

After church, I biked over to Vinny's to tell him the news.

"Man, two weeks to spend with the Irish Goddess." Vinny whistled. "I think I may have to sleep over."

I laughed. "I thought Tika was the Irish Goddess?"

Vinny was dribbling a basketball on his driveway. He was hoping to try out for the team next year in high school. "This town is big enough for two of them," he told me. He tossed the ball, and it went into the basket. "So tomorrow, you asking Kate out?"

I nodded. This was the last week of school. It was time.

The next day in school, I didn't run into Kate till lunchtime. She was sitting with Betsey, eating the pasta that was served that day. Luckily, I hadn't seen Tim or his jerk friends. Maybe they learned their lesson, I hoped.

"Hey, Morgan," Kate said, smiling at me. She had her long dark hair in a ponytail and was wearing a blue sweatshirt and jean shorts. She looked amazing. "Have a seat," she said.

"You really made Fat Willy cry?" Betsey asked, barely looking up from her lunch.

"Well, I had help," I told her, patting Kate on her shoulder.

"You just started a war," Betsey said, looking up and looking worried. "No fooling. Everyone is talking."

"Lay off, Bets," Kate said. "The war ended Saturday."

"Whatever," the blond girl said, carrying her tray away.

I was glad she left. I was nervous enough as it was, without having an audience. But I thought I might as well just go for it. Sort of like ripping a Band-Aid off fast. "I wanted to know if you wanted to go to the movies—" I began.

Kate interrupted me. "Yes."

I stopped and blinked. "Yes?"

She nodded and smiled. "Sure, it would be fun."

Damn, this is easy. Sara would be proud. I smiled at Kate. "My sister-in-law will drive us if that's cool."

"Sure," she said, squeezing my hand. "I'm looking forward to it."

It was a week away before she would disappear and life of myself, and my friends would be in the fight of our lives.

That Monday afternoon, Vinny, Andy, and I rode our bikes home from school and stopped to inspect a dead squirrel that had been run over by a car. Vinny began to try to do some wheelies on his beat-up Huffy, going down Miller Ave. Andy, not one to like to be showed off, peddled faster than Vinny and took his hands off the handlebars. "Oh crap!" he yelled to us. "No brakes."

I laughed and passed Vinny and tried a useless attempt of a pop wheelie. Vinny suddenly yelled. "No brakes," he shouted and flew past Andy and I.

"You dumbass," Andy yelled after him. "Try your own jokes."

"No," Vinny screamed. "I really don't have any brakes!"

Andy and I slammed on our "working" brakes and watched Vinny go faster down the hill, both of us realizing that the brakes on Vinny's bike finally gave out on one of the biggest hills in town.

Vinny's bike had definitely picked up speed as he rode further and further away from us. He barely missed a station wagon backing out of a driveway. Andy and I both swore at the same time and began to chase after our skinny friend.

Vinny had to be like doing two hundred miles per hour down the street, and so far, he hadn't killed himself. He carefully avoided a yellow cat that froze in fear in the middle of the street, dodged a few parked cars, and even kept his balance riding over a storm drain.

I kept thinking Vinny should crash purposely in a bush or try to crash on the grass in someone's front yard, but he could still get hurt that way. "What do we do?" yelled Andy as he pedaled even faster down the street.

I heard a horn behind us, and I looked back. Artie drove up next to us in his white pickup truck. "What are two micks doing?" he asked us out of the passenger side window.

"Vinny lost the brakes on his bike!" I yelled at him.

Artie slowed his truck to keep pace with us. "Nothing we can do about it now. Slow down, you two, or you will crash yourselves."

Andy and I stopped our bikes on the edge of the curb, and by the time Artie got out of his truck and joined us, Vinny was almost at the end of Miller Ave. By now, he had ridden up on the sideway, and I saw many people diving out of the way.

"Oh crap," muttered Artie.

Vinny was approaching the Nail It Hardware store, where there was a huge display of outdoor lawn furniture. Vinny crashed right into a few lawn chairs, and I saw him fly off his bike into the mess.

"Stupid ass," Artie muttered.

Two minutes later, the three of us arrived at the hardware store. It was a miracle, and Vinny only got just a few scratches. His beloved Huffy, though, was truly dead this time. The handlebars were bent, many spokes in the bike's wheel were broken, and the back tire was no longer attached to the bike. Vinny teared up a bit as Artie helped him throw the bike into a nearby dumpster. We all understood our friend. A death of a bike hurts!

That same day, while Vinny was doing his own version of Evil Knievel, Parley ran into Nick the Slick and Fat Willy, walking home from school. Parley had stayed after to play Dungeons & Dragons with some kids in the library. He was alone when they cornered him by the old farmhouse out on Chestnut Road.

Parley got in two good punches off Fat Willy. I would like to say that Parley kicked both of their butts. That my chubby friend sent both of them home, crying again. But I'm not telling a fictional story here. Life isn't like some comic book story where Green Lantern comes to save the day, or the weakest kid in school fights off the bullies all by himself. I would have liked to say that. But what happened was Willy and Nick beat Parley within an inch of his life.

Parley spent the last week of school at the hospital over at St. John's Bay. He had three bruised ribs, a left black eye, and a broken left arm. He wouldn't tell his father or Sheriff Foster who did it. He only told Vinny, Andy, and I when we went to go visit him. Vinny was pissed at Parley for not saying who beat him up. It was not ratting someone out, Vinny said to Parley as he sat on the hospital bed, signing Parley's cast. Parley shook his head. He thought if he said something, he would get it worse the next time. He begged and made us swear not to tell anyone who beat him up.

Chapter 10

T HE NEXT DAY, MY parents left early for the airport, and I
went off to school. Brett would be at my house by the time
school was out. Rumors were already flying around school of
what happened to Parley. But my friends and I kept our mouths shut
when we were asked about it.

Andy had lain awake most of the night, thinking of ways to get
back at Fat Willy and Nick the Slick. By noon that lunchtime, he sat
down next to me and told him it was time to get one of them back.
Andy took out something that was wrapped up in aluminum foil.
"Come with me," he said. I followed him and was surprised to see
him approach Fat Willy.

The fat kid was sitting by himself, chewing down on a Hostess
CupCake, and crumbs were falling on this white shirt from it. Willy
looked up. "Get lost, Donahue."

"I'm not here to fight, Will," Andy said. It was the first time I
ever heard my friend call the fat jerk by his real name. "I want to call
a truce. And since you love brownies," Andy said, laying the package
on the table in front of Willy, "you can have my dessert."

"What are you—" I began to protest.

"No, Morg," Andy said, patting my back.

"It's time we end this stupid feud. Talk to you later, Will," Andy
said and walked back to his table.

I stood, looking just as surprised as Willy for a few seconds.
Then the bully shrugged, opened the package, and began to stuff the

brownies in his mustard-covered mouth. I walked back to our table and sat next to Andy. "What the hell was that?" I asked him.

Andy grinned. "Sometimes, it is awesome having older brothers. Don't worry, Willy will get his in about an hour or so," he said, looking at his watch.

"I don't get it," I told him. I looked back over at Fat Willy, who was stuffing another brownie into his mouth.

"I think Willy is constipated, Morgan. So I put some Exlax into the brownies to help him out."

Andy told me after school that day that Willy ran out of English class about 2:05 p.m. holding his butt. He spent the rest of the afternoon in the boy's lavatory.

Brett and I had an awesome rest of the week together. We cooked dinner and joked around, listening to music. We watched movies and our favorite TV shows together. Since she had come to stay with me, I hadn't dreamt of Hazel since Sunday night.

School ended for us eighth graders that Friday afternoon, and we were going to have a graduation ceremony the next Friday.

Friday evening, my sister-in-law helped pick out what I should wear for my first date. I wore blue jeans, my new green Converse sneakers, and a light blue button-down shirt. I had to say to myself, I looked awesome. She drove me over to Kate's house, just a few blocks away, and then headed into town. She didn't ask Kate silly questions and let us off one block away from the movie theater.

I had told Brett that I was going to buy Kate ice cream after the movie so to pick us up at 9:30 p.m. We were going to see *Rocky 3* that had opened up a few weeks ago. Kate looked great in a yellow sundress and white Converse sneakers. I told you before, this fourteen-year-old had the body of a fifteen-year-old, and I couldn't stop looking at her.

We talked a little bit before the movie, and once it started, we giggled a few times but pretty much focused in on Rocky. We cried when Mick died and cheered when Mr. T got his ass kicked.

Afterward, we walked down Main Street to the ice cream shop, where we both got hot fudge sundaes. It was a really nice date, and Kate even kissed me on the lips real fast before Brett drove up.

Summer was here. School was out, at least for me and the eighth graders. The rest of the saps still had one more week of school. I slept till about ten that Saturday morning. Brett was laying on the couch, sipping coffee, and reading the Bridgeport post. She was wearing one of Tom's T-shirts, and her tanned legs looked fantastic.

"What's up, lover boy?" she grinned as I walked into the living room.

"Ha, ha," I said, blushing, and sat down by her feet.

"What do you have going on today?" she asked.

"Hang out," I said. "Supposed to meet Vinny, Andy, and um… Kate at the CCC about eleven."

"Oh, another encounter with the infamous Kate Sheppard," my sister-in-law said, giving me a soft kick in the chest. She sat up and folded the paper. "I got some writing to do, and then, Tika and I are doing lunch."

She sighed. "Tika ran into jerk head again last night. Had an argument outside of Sully's pub. Clinton is such an ass."

I had to agree with Brett. As I said before, Clinton Rushmore was a total dick. Thought he was the greatest cop in the world, plus he also dumped Tika and still treated her badly. "I'd love to kick his ass," I said.

I expected Brett to laugh, but she patted my legs. "You sure are growing up fast there, Morg." She got up and headed into the kitchen. "I'm going to hit the shower. Don't burn the town down."

I shook my head. Damn, I loved her.

Before heading downtown, I decided to go see little Christy Foster. I haven't seen her since Sara's funeral. Mrs. Foster was out on the front lawn, planting some yellow and red roses. She gave me hug and told me that Christy was out back, playing in the sandbox.

I found the blond six-year-old ankle deep in her square wooden sandbox that her father had built for her last summer. She had a few Matchbox cars in the sand and was driving them around. She jumped up and hugged me when I approached.

"How are you doing, kiddo?" I asked her.

"I'm good," she replied.

And she did look good and happy. Her blond hair was in pig-tails, and she had the cutest smile. But I'm sure it had to be hard for her, missing Sara and everything. I bent down next to her and played cars with her for a few minutes.

"Sara got deaded," she said after a while.

I looked at her and nodded.

"I hope I don't get deaded too."

I looked at her puzzled. "Why would you say that?" I asked her. "Nothing is going to happen."

She looked down at her cars. "All those other kids got tooken. They may be deaded too."

I sighed, not knowing what to say. I didn't want to lie or say something that could upset the girl. Christy was not just the sheriff's kid and knew what was going on in Penny's Creek, she was also very smart, like her sister. I turned her head to look at me. "It's true those kids are missing," I said. "But they may not be dead. Someone will find them."

Christy nodded. "Sara said that too. She told me she tried looking for them. Mr. Wire too."

I started to ask her what she meant by that when Mrs. Foster came around back and told Christy it was time for her lunch. I said goodbye to them both and promised to come by sometime next week.

I got to the CCC around eleven. Andy was there with Tinkerbelle and Kate. They were looking at the new gaming section that Artie and Tika had finally opened up. They had kiddie games like Chutes and Ladders and Candy Land. They had board games like Monopoly, Clue, Battleship, Operation, and a few chess sets. The shop now also had books, dice, and everything one would need to get started play-ing Dungeons & Dragons.

Artie was in his usual position, eating a burger with his legs up on the counter, and reading an *Incredible Hulk* comic. He looked up at me. "O'Riely, don't you have anything better to do than come here every day?"

"Nope," I said, giving him the finger and walking to the back of the store. Kate smiled at me. She was dressed in tan shorts, Keds sneakers, and a red checkered shirt. "Morning," I said to her.

She smiled and quickly brushed her hand with mine. I said hi to Andy and Jessica, and we talked about the games in the store, waiting for the late boy. Late boy was Vinny. We were always waiting for him. I wouldn't say he was a slowpoke, but he sure took his damn time. He was always late for school, to go to the movies, or to our houses to hang out. The worst was going to the arcade with him. His mom would drop us off for a few hours at the Milford Rec. I would play for an hour or so and then, be out of quarters. Parley, the cheap bastard, would bring a dollar with him and be out of money in like seven seconds. Vinny, on the other hand, could play an arcade game for like over an hour with just two quarters. He was damn good, but it sucked having to wait for him to get eaten by a ghost in Pac-man or crushed by Godzilla.

Skinny Vinny showed up about twenty minutes later, and we decided to picnic at the park and play hide-and-seek in the woods. We stopped off at the deli and got some sandwiches, pickles, Pepsi, and a bag of chips.

The day was sunny and warm and cloudless. The park wasn't very crowded since most of the kids were still in school. We talked about what high school would be like as we ate. Afterward, we threw out trash away and walked to the edge of the park, where the woods were. We did rock paper scissors to see who the seeker was. Andy lost.

As he began to count, I boldly grabbed Kate's hands, and we ran into the woods together, determined to find a good hiding spot. Vinny ran past, muttering that he was going to attempt to climb a tree. We ran amongst the tall pines, chestnut, and oaks and hid behind a fallen pine. We heard Andy counting in the distance, and we both giggled hoping he wouldn't find us first. We had a blast that afternoon. By three, we were pretty beat though and decided to play one more round. It was my turn, so I closed my eyes and counted to sixty.

Then, I was off to find my prey. I found Tinkerbelle within thirty seconds, lying behind a cluster of ferns. "Nice try, Jess," I said to her. That was when I heard a girl scream in the distance.

Tinkerbelle looked at me in fear. "That sounded like Kate."

The two of us quickly ran in the direction Kate yelled from. "Kate, you all right?" I shouted.

All I heard was a few birds chirping above us and a squirrel running up a tree. "Kate!" I shouted.

"What's going on?" Andy said behind us, scaring us half to death. "We're taking a time out?"

"Didn't you hear Kate scream?" Tinkerbelle asked, grabbing his hand.

Andy laughed. "She probably saw a snake. You know girls."

Tinkerbelle removed her hand and stared hard at him. "Oh really," she said. For your information I'm—"

I cut her off. "Kate!" I shouted again.

By now, Vinny came out from wherever he was hiding. He too heard Kate scream. "Let's split up and look around," he suggested.

Ten minutes later, I could find no trace of the Bronx Beauty. I was sitting on a fallen log, thinking what to do when Tinkerbelle and Vinny approached and sat next to me.

"Find anything?" Jessica asked.

I shook my head, my fear now growing worse now by the minute. We continued to call out to no avail.

"Maybe she went home," Vinny suggested.

"She wouldn't have done that," I told him. "Damn it, she was just here."

"Guys!" we heard Andy yell from the distance. We turned and he ran over to us. "She isn't back that way either."

"What should we do?" whispered Jessica.

I thought for a few seconds as I saw Andy start to unwrap a Hostess CupCake.

"Hey, when did you get that?" asked Vinny, looking at the delicious chocolate cake.

Andy pointed behind him. "I found it back there. Still unwrapped. Who would leave a perfectly good cupcake in the woods?"

It was then I had an idea what might be happening in our little town. I just wasn't sure about it yet. "Andy, you and Tinkerbelle head over to Kate's to make sure she isn't there. Vinny and I are going to the police station."

"Aren't we"—Andy paused for moment, taking a bite out of the cupcake—"jumping the gun a bit here? She could be messing around."

"No, damn it!" I yelled. "We all heard her scream. She wouldn't do that. Now, please do what I say." I started to walk back toward the park. Shortly after, I heard the others following.

After separating, Vinny and I ran through the park toward downtown. The police station wasn't too far from the park, and we reached it in less than five minutes. Clinton was just coming out of the doors when we ran up the steps.

"Clinton, something's wrong!" I shouted.

Clinton sighed and shook his head. "How many times have I told you jerks, it's Officer Rushmore."

"Whatever, Clinton," Vinny said. If anyone hated Clinton more, it was Vinny. As I said, my friend had a wicked crush on Tika Murphy and thought the world of her.

Clinton stepped up toward Vinny, as to scare him.

"We think there's been another kidnapping!" I shouted.

Clinton turned toward me quickly, his face showing a mixture of emotions. Whether it was fear, shock, or anger; I didn't try to comprehend. "Kate Sheppard has gone missing from the woods," I told him.

That was when Sheriff Foster exited the police station, and we quickly explained to him what happened. Within minutes, we were back at the edge of the woods with the sheriff, Clinton, Officer Duva, and a tall cop with fiery red hair.

We showed them the area where we were playing hide-and-seek. Sheriff Foster squatted down and studied the forest floor for a few minutes, stroking his mustache. "We better get the dogs out, Clinton. See if they can pick up a trace."

Clinton nodded and ran back out of the woods. Clinton was in charge of these special dogs and had tried before to locate the missing kids, but it turned up nothing. By now, Andy and Jessica had returned from Kate's house, informing us that she wasn't home. Sheriff Foster told us that we had better head on home and let the experts do this. I protested but the man wouldn't let us help.

Chapter 11

B Y 5:00 P.M. THAT afternoon, Kate Sheppard had not been found. My friends and I had stayed at the park the whole time, hoping for some news. By now, the rest of the police force had been called in. Clinton had returned from deep in the woods, telling the sheriff he and the dogs found nothing.

The sheriff found it strange that the dogs didn't pick up a scent and figured she may not be in the woods after all. He had the rest of his officers patrolling up and down every street and parking lot in town.

I sat on a nearby park bench, drinking some Hawaiian punch Brett had brought down. Brett was clearly upset too especially since it could have been anyone one of us. First Selectman Whitmore came down around five thirty to talk to the sheriff. Parley's father was fat, just like his son, and had the reddish cheeks I've ever seen. Parley had told me that they even get redder when his father loses his temper. I got off the bench and walked up behind them to listen.

"I told you that's it. Rushmore's dogs couldn't find a trace of her. She isn't in the woods. Have the men pull out. We still aren't sure that she is truly missing." Whitmore pointed over to my friends sitting at the table with Brett. "Just a bunch of kids saying she is missing after playing hide-and-seek."

The sheriff barely nodded and stared off into the woods.

Clinton walked up to the two of them and gave me a disgusted look. "I agree with the mayor, Will. She isn't out there."

"We will look for a couple more hours," Sheriff Foster said.

"You will do no such thing," Mayor Whitmore yelled. His cheeks getting red. "We don't need any more news vans coming into our little town. Hell, her parents haven't reported her missing yet."

The mayor failed to admit that Kate's parents were still at work in Hartford or on their way home. Parley's father took a deep breath. "Do as I say, Sheriff Foster, or this weekend will be your last." The mayor stormed off to his Cadillac and drove away.

"Okay," the sheriff said, and he said to Clinton, "Call the men back."

"What!" I shouted.

The sheriff turned, surprised to see me listening in. "Morgan, it will be all right. We will find her."

"No," I said, shaking my head. "She is out in those woods. You got to keep looking, Mr. Foster."

"You heard the mayor," Clinton said with a sneer.

"Bullshit," I shouted. Everyone around us stopped whatever they were doing and looked at us. The sheriff just stared at me as if wondering who I was. "That's a bullshit order, Sheriff, and you god-damn know it! This is the fifth kid missing now. You can't give up."

I paused for a second and then spoke again. "Sara wouldn't have."

There was complete silence around us, and then, the sheriff turned to Clinton. "Take the dogs out again. Go in another two miles. Bring Duva with you. Have rest of the men continue patrolling every inch of this town."

Clinton sighed. "Oh, come on, Will. I just pulled the men out. We aren't going—"

The sheriff cut him off. "No, go back out again."

Clinton gave me a look of hate and turned back to his boss "Will, I got a date tonight with that Spanish chick and—"

Sheriff Foster stepped right up to him and jammed his finger into the officer's chest. "Then I suggest you get looking, Clinton."

The sheriff looked at me, smiled, and walked over to his cruiser. I looked back at Clinton and wondered what the hell his problem was.

Clinton swore and spit on the ground. "It's useless, you little punk. You will never find her."

I walked back to my friend and told him what happened. I told Brett that I wanted to stay just for a bit longer. She agreed and head for home. After she left, I turned to Tinkerbelle, Andy, and Vinny. "We are going to find Kate and those other kids ourselves."

My friends followed me as I left the park and headed back downtown. I had a plan set in my mind, and I needed my friends' help to set it in motion.

"Dude, slow up," complained Vinny. "You're nuts if you think you can find the missing kids."

I kept walking. "The town had their chance," I said. "They didn't do squat. It's our turn now."

"So where are we going?" Andy asked. He was holding Jessica's hand. She had an anxious look and had barely spoken since Kate disappeared.

"We need a ride," I told him. I looked both ways and crossed over to Main Street. A few people on the street were already talking about the new missing kid.

"A ride?" Vinny asked. "Who?"

I didn't answer and kept on walking till we reached the CCC. Tika was behind the counter, smoking a cigarette and reading an *Incredible Hulk # 268*. Her cousin wasn't in the shop.

"What's wrong?" she immediately asked, knowing us so well.

I quickly told her about Kate's disappearance and that it seemed the police, especially Clinton, were doing a half-ass job going about it.

The redhead let out a puff of smoke and swore under her breath. "Clinton is Penny Creek's definition of an asshole," she said. "Never knew why I dated him."

"You can always date me," Vinny spoke up.

"We need a ride to Daniel's Junction," I said as Tika put out her cigarette.

She looked at me for a few seconds with her mouth open and then yelled. "What! I don't think so, Morgan O'Riely." She shook her head furiously and pointed toward the door. "That maniac probably is still out there in the woods."

Vinny, Andy, and even Jessica began shouting at me. Telling me it was a really bad idea to go hiking through the woods looking for Kate.

"Besides," Andy said. "Clinton had his dogs out there twice. They didn't pick up a scent of any of the kids."

I shook my head. I didn't care whether Clinton and his mangy dogs had not picked up a scent. I just knew Kate and maybe the other kids were out there somewhere. "I know who is taking the kids," I said.

Everyone stopped talking and looked at me as if I told them I knew who shot John F. Kennedy. There was complete silence in the CCC. Tika's cigarette ash had stopped smoking, and the *Hulk* comic dangled from her fingertips. Vinny and Andy just stared, and Tinkerbelle looked at me with a puzzled expression and was scratching her short blond hair looking a lot like Stan Laurel.

"It's Fat Willy."

Andy shook his head, and I saw him trying to hide his smile. "You're telling me that the fattest teen in town is the one taking all these kids? That's impossible. No way."

I shrugged. "I don't have exact proof just yet, except for that Hostess CupCake you found."

"That doesn't prove anything, Morgan," Vinny stated. He sat up on the counter and folded his arms. "So there was a cupcake wrapper. Willy is not the only one to eat those in town. Those cupcakes rule."

"I know," I responded. "It's also what Parley told me in the hospital when we visited him last. When you guys went to the soda machine, Parley told me something Willy had said when Slick Nick and Willy were beating him up. Willy said that Parley was going to disappear just like all the other kids."

"Still," Andy said, looking disgusted. "Doesn't mean much."

"Listen, you can come with me or not." I turned back to Tika. "I need your help. Take me out to the edge of Daniel's Junction."

"If you think I'm taking you out into the woods two hours before darkness, you are sadly mistaken, my short Irish friend," Tika said. "Brett will have my ass. She is responsible for you while your folks are away."

She got up out of her chair. "Let the sheriff and his men do their jobs."

"I'm not losing Kate like we lost Sara!" I shouted. "No way, goddamn it." I walked to the door of the shop expecting a long walk to the woods.

"You suck sometimes!" Tika said, slamming her hands on the counter and spilling a collection of *Choose Your Own Adventure* books onto the floor. She shook her head and swore under her breath. "Okay, fine."

I smiled at her. "Thank you. Be ready in an hour. Now, are you guys helping or not?"

Vinny shrugged and held up his hands in defeat. "It's a fool's mission, but whatever. I'm in."

"So am I." Andy sighed, clearly acting like this was the dumbest idea he ever heard of. "Besides, you will need my strength."

Jessica nodded. "Let's go find them."

"Okay, Tinkerbelle, you and Andy go on over to Parley's. We need his help."

"Uh, news flash, Morgan. Parley can't come out to play," Andy said as he thumbed through one of the adventure books. "Boy has gotten a broken arm." He tossed the book back on the ground and grabbed a Hershey's bar off the candy display.

He saw Tika eyeing him. "What? I'm hungry. Need energy for Morgan's big expedition into the deep woods of Penny's Creek."

"Don't be an asshole, Andy," Jessica said. "At least Morgan is doing something."

Andy looked as he was going to argue but he turned away instead and bit into the candy bar. "Why do you need Parley?"

"His father owns the sporting goods store over in St. John's, right? Parley showed me all of this hiking and camping equipment. A lot they store in their basement at the house. We need flashlights and compass and you know…like hiking stuff. Maybe some canteens."

Everyone agreed that was a good idea.

I continued. "We will meet back here in an hour. Grab a sweat-shirt and some blankets too. We may need them." I poked Vinny in the arm. "You come with me."

The two of us left the CCC before the others asked where we were going. We headed back toward the creek near Sara's house.

"So what are we doing?" Vinny asked.

"To get the last member of our search party," I told him.

Vinny ran up to catch up to me. "Who?" he asked. "Where the hell are we going?

"We're going to find Haywire."

It was going on about six when we reached our hideout behind Sara's house. I could hear Christy playing in her backyard, and I really missed Sara at that moment. She would have known what to do. Sara Foster always had a plan. I had a half-assed plan but really had no clue what I was doing, but I had to find Kate.

I was pretty sure Haywire knew what was going on in Penny's Creek. I think he and Sara had discussed it actually. I was betting on help from the town crazy. But I remembered all the times I ran into Haywire the last few weeks, and we all thought the man was shouting incoherent babble. But Haywire knew. He had said that woods had them.

"So now what?" Vinny asked, sitting down on his favorite gray rock. The water in the creek was running strong, and the sounds of the water cascading over the stones. Along with the birds singing, it made the late afternoon seem peaceful. But somewhere out in the woods were Kate and probably the other missing kids.

"The woods have another one," a voice said from behind us.

Vinny was startled and almost pitched forward off the rock he was sitting on. "Geesh, Haywire, give a guy a warning when you approach him."

Haywire, despite his wild appearance such as unkempt hair, torn red T-shirt, and patch-ridden black pants; the crazy man some-how maintained cleanliness. His gray hair was wet and combed back, and he had a Band-Aid on his cheek. "I saw you at the park," he said to me. "You were there with your friends and the one that roars."

Vinny's mouth dropped open in awe at the strangeness of Haywire. My friend looked over at me and mouthed "The one that roars?"

I shrugged. Who knew what Haywire meant half the time? The dude lived in the woods and probably ate bugs. I just focused on what he had said about the woods. He was a tall man, but as I said before, everyone was taller than me, including Hefty Smurf. "Do you know where Kate Sheppard is?" I asked.

Haywire nodded. "It is damp and dark, but there is fire."

Vinny grunted. "Shit, Morgan, the man is looney tunes. A combo of Daffy Duck and Jan Brady."

"Shh," I said to Vinny. "Haywire, what do you mean? I need to know where the kids are." I grasped his arm firmly but gently. "Please."

The man nodded. "I will show you, Morgan. They are deep in the woods with the one that roars and the candy eater."

Vinny sucked in his breath. "Fat Willy."

As we walked onto Edison Road, we saw a police car pass us with the lights on, doing street-by-street searches as Sheriff Foster requested. Parley's father was so stupid to think that Kate was somewhere in town.

Coming around the corner, we almost ran into Tim White walking his dog, Lucifer. Lucifer began to wag his tail at the sight of me. I wanted to bend down and scratch his head but was afraid how Tim might react.

Tim looked surprised as we did, but Vinny suddenly got angry and moved up to the bully. "Where the hell is Fat Willy!" he demanded. "He took Kate and—"

Tim gave Vinny a small shove. "Back off, Catalano. What are you jabbering about?"

Tim looked at me with a fierce look. He looked over at Haywire, and I could see the puzzlement on his face why we were with the town crazy.

I wanted to confront Tim White right then. After all, he was best friends with Fat Willy, but I didn't have any real proof that he was really taking the kids. Plus, I couldn't afford to get into an all-out brawl with the town bully at the present time.

"Kate Sheppard has gone missing," I said and quickly told him what happened, starting off with us playing hide-and-seek and finishing with us heading into the woods. I left out the part of Willy possibly being involved.

Tim White squatted down and patted Lucifer. "Damn, Kate is a real cutie too. I will keep my eyes open." He gave Vinny a harsh look, and they walked off down the street.

"He may know something, Morgan," Vinny protested. "He has to—"

I cut him off. "There is no time to question him now. Come on, the others are waiting for us."

Chapter 12

WE ALL PILED INTO Tika's red Jeep in front of the CCC. I sat up front, sharing a seat with Vinny while Andy, Tinkerbelle, Parley, and Haywire sat in the back. Tika had been muttering how stupid this was and why she was doing this.

Jessica, sitting on Andy's lap next to Haywire, sat still as if she was playing freeze tag. Again, Haywire was harmless, but he was the town crazy and one did not pursue a friendship with him. It was sad actually.

We barely spoke on our way to Daniel's Junction, which was where many hiking trails branched off from. From these trails, one could venture deep into the woods.

Parley looked a lot better than he did in the hospital, but his left arm was still in a cast and sling. Andy didn't want him to go with us, but Parley insisted on coming; otherwise, he wouldn't give us the supplies.

The seven of us each had a flashlight, a canteen of water, and a sweatshirt. Haywire had on a pink gray sweatshirt of Artie's that Tika had found in the back of the shop. He looked pretty funny in the "One Day at a Time" sweatshirt, showing Schneider the handyman. Why Artie had that pink sweatshirt was beyond me, and I was pretty sure we were going to break his balls one day if we survived.

Andy and I both had backpacks, with a few blankets, matches, a cord of rope, a first aid kit, beef jerky, and some Twinkies that Parley insisted on bringing. It was after 6:25 p.m. when Tika pulled her Jeep onto the small lot off Route 27. From there, we were going to follow Haywire to God only knew where.

Andy had tried questioning him on how Fat Willy was doing all the kidnappings, but Haywire just stared off into space.

The woods were loud with birds chirping and the occasional animal heard running through the woods. Huge tall pine trees and scattered oaks and pines covered the trial. Parley and Andy were having an argument whether Charles Ingalls was nosey or not.

"Listen, Parley," Andy said, tossing small stone up and down. "Charles is always getting into everybody's business. Missing Orphan; Charles's business."

Andy threw the stone up again. "Nels getting bossed around by Harriet; freaking Charles's business again. Drunken farmer," Andy paused and said nothing for a few seconds and grinned. "Charles's business."

He tossed the stone as hard as he could into the woods. "I mean, come on, Ingalls."

Parley protested. "On the show last night, that drunk was being mean to his kids. Charles had to get involved."

"By kicking his ass?" Andy asked.

"Hey, *Little House on the Prairie* is always better when there is action like a fight," Vinny added. "I love it when Ingalls kicks butt."

I didn't see last night's episode, but I had to agree with Vinny. You can say what you want about Charles Ingalls, but the man loved to fight.

Jessica didn't say much but hummed a song as she walked beside Andy. Tika had a determined look on her face. I moved up next to her.

"Tell me why I am doing this?" she asked, brushing her curly red hair out of her eyes.

"'Cause you love me," I said.

"That I do, my fellow Irish friend," she said, smiling over at me. "You know when Brett finds out, we are both dead."

We walked for a good half hour or so before Haywire held up his hand. He was staring off the west side of the woods of the trail. I looked up and saw the sun rapidly descending over the forest ceiling. It was starting to get a bit cold and a slight wind had picked up.

Haywire looked at me and pointed into the woods. "The hole is there."

Everyone looked at each other, shrugging.

"What do you mean hole?" Tika asked. She walked to the edge of the trail and looked where the man was pointing.

She moved her hands in the air. "All I see are woods and like more woods."

"They keep them there," Haywire told her. "Old mine."

He turned and saw us watching him for an explanation. Haywire then spoke the most words I or maybe the whole town of Penny's Creek ever heard him speak. "An old abandoned mine is out there. Overgrown now. Few know about it. That's where they are."

Jessica began to shout. "Are you saying you knew the whole time where the kids are? Why didn't you do something or tell someone, you crazy old jerk!"

Andy moved over and put his arm over her shoulder. "Easy. It's not his fault."

I sighed expecting the worst. "Come on," I said, adjusting my backpack. "Show us the old mine, Haywire."

We walked a good three-fourth of a mile on what looked like what used to be a trail, but long ago, the woods had taken it over. We all, by now, had broken out our flashlights to light our way through the approaching darkness.

"How do we know he isn't just leading us to a hidden place to slaughter us?" Parley whispered. He was huffing and puffing and probably haven't had walked this much in his entire life. "Go all Leatherface on our asses."

"You watch too many horror movies," I told the mayor's son.

And at that, Penny's Creek town crazy called us to a halt. "In there," he said, pointing toward the ground.

We all looked to where Haywire was pointing. It kind of looked like a well. A few stones made a circular pattern in the ground, and they were stacked about a foot high. We stood at the edge and shined our flashlights down into the darkness. It wasn't really a well, though. The hole was at least three feet in diameter and sloped off to the left.

"The mine," Haywire whispered.

We all jumped at the sound of an owl in the distance, and Tinkerbelle giggled, breaking our nervousness.

"If you knew the kids were down there," Andy said, moving besides Haywire, "why the hell didn't you do something?"

Just before, he had stopped Jessica from freaking out on the man, but now, he was doing the same thing. Andy grabbed the man by his arm and began to shake him. "Why didn't you do something?"

Haywire shoved Andy back and shook his head. "I tried. I told him. The one that roars but he didn't listen and locked me up instead."

Andy saved himself from almost falling down and looked at me in disbelief. "You're saying…you told Sheriff Foster about this?"

We all kept silent as Haywire glanced at all of us. "I have to brush my teeth," he said simply and then walked off into the darkness.

"Where the hell are you going!" Andy screamed and started after the old man. I grabbed hold of him though and told him to let him go.

"Morgan, he knows," Vinny said, pointing down into the hole. "He knew."

"Nothing we can do about it now," Tika said. "Haywire brought us here. Now, let him be." The redhead started toward the hole as if to climb in.

"What are you doing?" I asked, letting go of Andy.

She looked up at me and brushed a curl of hair out of her eyes. "I have to see what's down there. You guys stay here and wait while I take a look."

Vinny moved up next to her. "I'm coming with you."

She shook her head. "You stay. I want to see if there is anything down here." She bent down and shined her light into the hole. "The tunnel does go off to the left," she stated. Tika moved her legs over the edge of the hole and prepared to jump down.

"Tika, don't," I said. I was suddenly very scared. I wanted to be back at home, drinking a Pepsi and playing chess with Brett or watching a rerun of *M*A*S*H*. The early seasons though with Trapper, Henry, and Frank Burns. The new ones were a bore fest! I began to think I made a mistake coming out here, and I was afraid of what Tika may find down in that hole or mine or whatever Haywire claimed it to be.

Tika looked up at me with those magnificent green eyes of hers, and I could see that she was plenty scared, but she was one of the bravest people I ever knew. I knew she was going to do it no matter what. The redhead grasped my hand and smiled. "It's going to be okay. Just give me about twenty minutes."

"Us twenty minutes," Vinny said, also moving his legs over to the edge of the hole. He saw the disapproval on Tika's face. "You always said don't go anywhere by yourself."

Tika was quiet for a moment and let out a deep sigh. It was very hard to argue with Vinny Catalano, and Tika knew that better than anyone. "Fine, I go first. The rest of you wait here for twenty minutes. If we don't come back, then head back and get help."

She tossed her car keys to me and I caught them. She dropped down into the hole and off down the slope and disappeared. Vinny quickly followed behind. Shortly after, the lights from their flashlights had gone away, and the last I heard was Tika yelling for Vinny to quit staring at her ass.

Jessica and Parley had been silent the whole time before Tika went down into the hole and keep silent until ten minutes passed. It was Parley who started the trouble first. "Time is up," he said, glancing at his left wrist that didn't even contain a watch. "Let's head on out."

I looked up at him. "It's been barely ten minutes, Parley. She said twenty," I reminded him. I could see my chubby friend was getting anxious, and it was pretty dark in the woods by now. Luckily, the moon was almost full, so we could see each other by moonlight.

"It feels like it's been twenty minutes," Jessica said, twirling her hair again.

"We wait," I told her.

Parley moved toward me. "Either way, it's been a long time. Let's head back to the road. Andy can drive Tika's Jeep. She let him drive a few times." Parley laughed for a second.

"Remember, she let you drive down in Harper's field, and you almost hit that wooden fence."

Andy kept silent, sitting on a fallen oak. He was munching on a twig and shining his light down the hole.

Parley suddenly grabbed the Jeep's keys out of my hands and stuck them into his pockets. "We are leaving."

"Hey!" I protested. "What do you think you are doing?"

"He's right, Morgan. It's time to leave," Tinkerbelle said. She had quit playing with her blond hair and stood defiantly beside Parley.

I didn't know what to say or do. I looked over at Andy who still hadn't moved or said a word since Tika and Vinny went on their special mission. All I heard were the crickets in the darkness and that annoying owl that wouldn't shut the hell up.

"Are you coming are not?" Parley said. He looked really mean at the moment, his broken arm and all, staring at me as if I was scum for wanting to stay.

"We are staying," I said simply.

"You are staying, we are leaving," Parley said and began to walk slowly back down the broken path. "Get walking, Andy," he said over his shoulder.

Jessica walked over to Andy and patted him on his back. He nodded at her, stood up, and tossed the stick he was chewing on the ground.

"Andy," I said. I couldn't believe he was leaving too. I didn't want to stay out here in the woods myself, and besides, Tika and Vinny needed us.

"They are our friends, damn it!" I shouted.

"Come on," Jessica said, grabbing onto Andy's hand.

"Sorry," Andy said looking over at me. "We can't leave them."

"Oh, this is such bullshit," Parley said in the darkness.

Andy suddenly hugged Tinkerbelle for a few seconds and brushed her short blond hair with his hands. "You go on back and find help. Morgan and I are going down into the mine."

She didn't protest but hugged him back and then walked back to Parley. Right then, I knew our friendship was dead with Parley. At least, my friendship was. I jumped down into the hole after Andy.

Chapter 13

NDY AND I CRAWLED in silence for a bit. I heard him breathing in front of me and the soft sounds of our hands and knees hitting the packed dirt. Every few seconds, Andy would shine the flashlight down in the tunnel, and all we saw was darkness. The tunnel could go for like a mile or just another hundred yards. We didn't know, and the only choice was to keep on trekking. I kept thinking if this was truly where the kids had been brought to, it sure was a crappy and inconvenient way to bring them.

But then, the tunnel seemed to get wider, and we were able to almost stand up and squat as we walked. In the distance, I heard the sound of wind and then, felt a gentle breeze on my face.

"You feel that?" Andy asked me.

I nodded, forgetting I was behind him and couldn't see me, but Andy kept moving on down the tunnel.

Suddenly, he stopped and I bumped into him. "Hey," I said, "what gives?"

"I thought I heard something."

I listened for a few seconds but heard nothing except for the wind and my increased heartbeat. "What did you hear?" I asked.

He turned and looked at me with the light shining on his face. "I think I heard a kid scream." Andy looked scared, and I don't think I ever saw Andy Donahue scared before. Not during the dirt rock fight, not with the fights between Fat Willy, and not even the time his dad caught him drinking a beer in the garage. I figured it had to come from years of getting his ass kicked in by older siblings. But yes, Andy was scared, and that made me even more afraid.

"Let's keep moving," I said.

We kept on moving on for about three more minutes when we both saw a faint glow of light further down the tunnel. As we moved on, the light grew even brighter. The tunnel grew wider and higher as well, and then, we stumbled out into a huge cave.

The cave was the size of the CCC. About a dozen torches sticking out of the walls of the cave, and its ceiling was at least twenty feet high. The light coming from the torches threw shadows on the walls, and it didn't quite reach the back of the cave. The floor had cracks and holes where one had to be careful walking on or they could stumble and break an ankle.

Beer and soda cans, candy wrappers, and some Hostess CupCake wrappers were scattered about the floor of the cave. And standing in the middle of the cave, holding onto a boy's left arm, was Fat Willy. He looked just as surprised as we were.

The bully was dressed in his usual messy clothing, and he had a cigarette in his free hand.

The kid he was holding onto was about nine and was dressed only in shorts. He looked dirty and tired. I knew him at once, Ben Jackson, the albino kid that went missing a few weeks ago.

"What in the hell?" muttered Fat Willy. He let go of the little kid, sending him falling onto the ground.

Andy and I both looked at each other, not knowing what to say or do. Do we rush the fat jerk and beat the hell out of him? Or do we run for help? We got our answer though as we heard a struggle from the left part of the cave. Suddenly, Vinny came stumbling out of the darkness into the light and fell down hard.

"Run," he muttered, looking up at us as blood trickled out of a bad cut on his left cheek.

Before we could do anything, Officer Clinton Rushmore stepped up beside Vinny. The police officer had one arm around Tika's neck, and in the other, he had a handgun pointing at the red-head's chest.

"You lied to me, Tika!" he shouted. He shoved his gun deeper into her belly. "You told me it was just you and the skinny asshole."

It was then, I realized who Haywire had been talking about, "The one who roars." It was Clinton. The jerk was always yelling at everyone, and I had seen him do it many times to the town crazy. Yelling at him to get off the street, yelling at him to clean himself, or yelling at him for helping an old lady across the street.

Fat Willy, by now, moved over about five feet away from us, and he was holding a huge knife. The kind Michael Myers was fond of. The albino kid had crawled away from him. Willy also held a kerosene lantern, which threw out more light than any of the torches combined. We were able to see the rest of the cave.

About thirty feet away sat a girl about twelve and besides her, knelt Kate Sheppard. At least I thought it was her. The older girl had a black bandana wrapped around her head, blinding her. "Kate!" I shouted, moving toward her but Willy waved the knife at me.

"Morgan," Kate barely whispered as she turned her head toward me frantically.

Clinton shoved Tika down on the ground. Vinny reached over and pulled her close to him. As I said, Tika was a tough girl, and so far, tears hadn't spilled out of her, but I knew that was fast approaching.

"Clinton!" she yelled. "What have you done to these poor children!"

She moved to shove Clinton, but he stepped out of the way. "I don't think so, red." It was then I noticed that the cave was cold. I saw the albino kid, the girl, and Kate shivering. Their clothes were dirty, and Kate seemed to be soaking wet. A cold breeze came from the right side of the cave.

"You are so dead, Willy," growled Andy.

"Yeah, you fat bastard," muttered Vinny from the ground and then, let out a grunt of pain as Willy kicked him in the stomach.

"Everyone shut up!" yelled Clinton. "I'm trying to have some fun here."

He reached down and hauled up Tika, whose eyes were now showing clear terror. He looked as if he was going to slap her. But then, calmness appeared on his face. "Baby doll," he said in a soft voice. "I'm sorry for hitting you before. But you were being a woman."

He turned and looked at his fat partner. "You know women never ever shut up," he said. He nudged his gun into Tika's chest. "Now, calm down and listen."

"Just tell me why, Clinton," Tika said. "Why are you doing this?"

Clinton looked dumbstruck for a moment and looked at the group of kids around him. Vinny had sat up and was trying to stop the flow of blood from his wound. He looked like he was about twenty seconds away from trying to fight Clinton. Andy and I stood side by side, covered by the fattest kid in town, who had the biggest knife in town. As for the kidnapped kids, all I could see were Kate, the albino kid, who had crawled over to her; and the girl still crying next to her.

Clinton shrugged. "Ehh, because we can."

It was then I realized there was true evil in this world. Clinton and Willy had taken these kids away from their families and did God-knows-what to them in this cave in the woods of Penny's Creek. And it was for no reason at all. Lex Luthor, Darth Vader, and Charles Manson couldn't hold a candle to this evil duo.

"You didn't make them do—" Tika began as tears began to stream down her face.

Clinton looked disgusted. "What? Something sexual? What the hell, Tika, you think I'm some kind of sicko?" He looked over at Willy and nodded. "We just played a few torture games with them is all."

Willy protested. "And those two that died, we didn't make them."

Andy shoved into Willy, sending him stumbling back, dropping the lantern. Luckily, it fell right side up and didn't break. Willy lashed out with the knife cutting into Andy's chest as he screamed in pain. Andy went down to his knees holding his chest.

"Damn it, Will," Clinton said, moving his pistol through his blond hair. "If I have told you once, I told you thousands of times, take...your...time." He then kicked Vinny in the face as he was about to launch himself at the officer.

Tika continued to struggle as Clinton looked back at her. "Now first, I want to have some fun with my ex-girlfriend here. It's been a while." His hand moved toward her breasts.

That was when the shotgun went off, startling everyone. The echoes of the blast sounded off every wall of the cave. Then, there was complete silence as we heard footsteps on the small stones on the cave floor. I heard a deep growl, and then, two figures stepped into the light.

Tim White and his Doberman pinscher, Lucifer, stood staring at us. Tim was dressed in his usual threads: jeans and a tight T-shirt. He held a shotgun in his hand. No one spoke for a few second until Clinton broke the silence.

"Who in the—" Clinton said, taking a step forward toward Tim.

"The name's Tim White," the town bully said, and then, he cocked his shotgun, sending the sound echoing off the cave's wall again.

He pointed the shotgun at us. "And it all ends now."

Chapter 14

WE WERE ALL STUNNED into silence for a few moments. All I heard was the wind passing through the cave and a few growls from Lucifer. Not even the kidnapped kids made a sound. Somewhere in the back of the cave, I could hear water dripping off the cave walls. I didn't know what to do. My greatest enemy was standing before me with a shotgun, and I knew I was seconds away from certain death.

Fat Willy let out a whoop and clapped his hands. "Awesome, Timmy boy!" He waved his knife around in the air. "I knew it all along."

Tim spit on the ground and didn't move the gun that he still had pointed at us. But his eyes moved over to Willy. "Knew what?"

"That Clinton and I could count on you," Willy told his friend. "O'Riely here and company think they are here to mess everything up. Stupid jerks. It is time for you to get even with them. I know you have been counting on it, Tim. Now, I knew that—"

"Shut the hell up, fatso," Tim muttered, moving that shotgun a few inches toward Wily. "You sick twisted psycho."

"Ease up there, Timmy," Clinton said, letting go of his ex-girlfriend. Tika fell onto her knees hard, letting out a grunt. I could see one of her knees had started to bleed through a torn hole in her jeans. "You got this all wrong."

Tim shook his head. "No, you got it all wrong, Office Rushmore. Now, shut up."

Tim looked over at me. "You okay, Morgan?" he asked.

I think I nodded but I was so confused I don't remember. I didn't know what was going on. Minutes ago, I had thought I had led my friends to certain death, and now, it seemed that we were about to be rescued.

"Vinny, help the redhead up. Andy and Morgan, go on help Kate and the kids," Tim told us.

"You kids move one inch, I will kill Tika right now," Clinton said, pointing his pistol back at the comic shop owner.

"I have no idea why you are here, White, but you made one bad mistake tonight," he sneered at Tim.

Tim stared right back at Clinton. "I said, don't move. Believe me, I know how to use this."

Fat Willy slammed his foot down. "You are being so stupid, Tim," he said. He waved his knife in the air. "You hate these punks just as much as me. Heck, you helped beat them up many times."

Tim nodded and moved a step backward. "That's true, Willy. Beating up kids and taking their money is one thing," Tim answered.

He shook his head slowly, and I could have sworn his eyes were tearing up. "Torturing and killing are very different, man. I have always known you were messed up!"

"The dude is a sick mother," Vinny added, who, by now, somehow got Tika back on her feet without Clinton noticing. My skinny friend held her hand tight. Any other time, Vinny would be in heaven holding his dream girl's hand, but now, it was a different matter entirely.

Clinton didn't seem to notice. He just kept staring at Tim as if he was just waiting for something to happen. I couldn't tell if the policeman was afraid or not, but to see Lucifer growling would frighten any man, though I knew the Doberman wouldn't harm a fly. Well, at least, I didn't think so.

I felt a small punch in my arm, and I realized that Andy was tugging me toward Kate and the kids. *Kate!* I thought suddenly.

I had forgotten all about her for a few moments. The young girl had taken Kate's blindfold off. Kate stood with her each of her arms over the girl's and the albino kid's shoulders.

Andy and I moved slowly over behind Clinton toward Kate as she began to move toward as us well, bringing the children with her.

"How did you find us by the way?" I heard Clinton ask.

"Haywire showed me. I had a feeling Willy was involved in these kids disappearing for a while now. I knew he had to have help from someone else too. Someone like you, Clinton."

Clinton laughed. "Well, being a cop gives me some power, lots of opportunity. Why do you think those dogs never picked up a trace of the kids in the woods? They did, of course, but I sure didn't tell the high and mighty sheriff that."

I had reached Kate, and she hugged me hard, almost knocking me over. She was breathing shallowly.

"Yeah, but you suck as a cop. You didn't even know I followed you to the cave entrance."

Andy looked over at me and mouthed, "Cave entrance?"

I shrugged. Leave it to the town crazy to bring us to the back door. That was when I saw Vinny take something out of his short pockets. It was too dark to see what he was doing, but I hoped he had some kind of plan to get out of this mess.

"Come on, kid," Clinton said, moving toward Tim. "You are not going to shoot anyone."

"I mean it, Clinton!" Tim shouted. "Don't move."

Lucifer started to bark fiercely as I saw Willy raise his knife in the air. That was when Vinny threw, whatever it was in his hand, hard at Clinton. I heard the coins fall to the ground as Clinton swore. Vinny had thrown the last of the $20 he had found back at the end of spring in that vacant lot. It had to be a few dollars, all in coins, because Clinton had cried out in pain.

Fat Willy prepared to throw his knife when Andy hurled himself at the fat boy's legs, knocking the evil jerk to the ground. I expected an earthquake as Willy hit the cave floor, but all that happened was he dropped his weapon.

Clinton and Tim both fired their guns at the same time. Tim's shot totally missed Clinton and but blew off Fat Willy's right hand instead. Clinton's bullet had hit Tim in his chest. As he fell over,

Lucifer leapt into the air, crashing into Clinton. The cop fell backward as Lucifer sank his teeth into Clinton's neck.

I'm not sure who was screaming louder; Clinton, as Lucifer went to town on the kidnapper's neck or Willy, who was on his knees, staring at what was left of his right hand or the rest of us. Tika had run over to Tim and knelt down by him.

"Come on, let's go now!" Andy said, moving toward the area of where Tim had come from. The young girl and the albino began to follow them when they began to scream louder as someone else appeared out of the darkness.

"Jessica!" Andy shouted as he recognized the short blond.

I'm not sure what she said to him, but she then began to scream at the carnage that was going on around us. I couldn't imagine the shock Tinkerbelle was feeling, but she was a little late for the party, and I didn't have time to calm her down. I moved over toward Tika, who was still kneeling next to Tim. Her hands were smeared with blood as she uselessly tried to stop the flow of blood from Tim's chest. But he was already dead.

Suddenly, I heard a yelp and saw that Clinton had somehow thrown the Doberman pinscher off him and was now kicking the dog in its side. Clinton was a huge guy, and if I went over to try to stop him, he would have smashed me to the ground as well. But Tika had another idea. She slowly walked over to the kerosene lantern that was still laying on the cave floor. She picked it up and held it over her head.

"Hey, lover boy!" she shouted.

The police officer/murderer/ex-boyfriend kidnapper/asshole looked over and smiled even though blood was pouring out of his neck wound. "You're next, red," he said.

Tika hurled the lantern. It seemed to flow into the air in slow motion, like a softball player's pop up out over center field. But then, the lantern came down and shattered onto Clinton's head. Flames burst out, engulfing him instantly. He looked like Johnny Storm, the Human Torch from the Fantastic Four. Only Johnny never screamed, unlike Clinton who screamed like I never heard a scream before.

"We got to go!" Vinny said, pulling on Tika who was transfixed on her burning ex-boyfriend. The cave was filling up with smoke, and we had to get out fast.

Lucifer had gotten back to his feet and began to bark as he ran to the side of the cave where he and his former master had appeared before. He kept turning back to look at us.

It was insane but it looked like he was telling us to follow him. I've seen my share of *Lassie and Benji* films. "Follow that dog!" I shouted, feeling like a complete idiot.

Andy was pretty much dragging Jessica, who had still been screaming. The girl was going to have nightmares for a while about this, I was sure. Kate had the two younger kids by the hand and ran after Andy. "Morgan, come on!" she shouted.

I nodded and took one last look at Tim lying on the floor and Clinton who, by now, had stopped shouting but was still burning. And Willy who had become—Willy! I had all but forgotten about him. The fat fourteen-year-old had become silent. He was still clutching his ruined right hand, and he must have gone into shock or something.

I felt a tap on my shoulder. "Come on, Morgan," Vinny said with Tika standing beside him. "This place is burning up."

I looked around. Sure enough, the flames from Clinton had spread to the various food wrappers and items on the cave floor. There must have been some flammable liquid on the cave floor because the flames continued to increase. I heard Lucifer barking in the distance and the yells from my friends.

"We can't leave him," I said, pointing down at Fat Willy who looked up at us with an innocent look.

"Are you insane, you idiot? He's the reason for all this!" Vinny protested.

I coughed, trying to not inhale any more smoke. "He is the reason, but now, Clinton is dead and so is Tim. We leave Willy to burn, we are no better than he is."

Vinny answered me by helping me haul the evil jerk up, with Tika's help. We dragged him out of the smoke, ridden cave, and found a passageway that was about fifty long. Somewhere, Tika had picked up a flashlight and led us outside into the woods.

The cave entrance was surrounded by five or six fallen pine trees that if you weren't looking for it, there would be no way to see the entrance. How Clinton had known about the cave, along with Tim, was beyond me. Andy was a few feet away, squatting down, talking to the boy and the girl. Lucifer was licking the little girl's face. Kate stood by Jessica who had a blank look on her face.

I wasn't sure how long we were in the cave, but it had to be early in the morning hours now. The woods were filled with crickets and a few hoots from owls. It would have been a perfect night for camping.

"So what now?" Vinny asked me. The bright moon shined down through the forest ceiling, and I saw that his face was dirty. I looked at the rest of us, and we looked the same. We were covered in cave dirt, sweat, and smoke. But Kate and the kids looked the worst. They looked super skinny and exhausted. It would be some time before they would look clean and healthy again.

I shrugged as Kate walked up to me. "You okay?" I asked her.

She then threw her hands around me and began to sob uncontrollably. I guess there are times that words don't need to be said. I had no idea what happened in that cave, and I was too scared to find out.

Fat Willy had passed out on his back, still clutching his bleeding hand, where, now, Tika was wrapping the wound with a piece of her torn shirt.

That was when I heard voices in the darkness, and then, lights from flashlights fast approaching from the north. "Tika!" We heard a voice from a bull horn sound. Then, my name was called out.

It was help! We all began to shout at once as the voices rapidly approach us. It was Sheriff Foster, Officer Duva, and two other police officers, along with Haywire and Brett.

"Morgan!" my sister-in-law shouted and almost tripped over a few branches rushing over to me. She grabbed me and held me close and kept kissing me all over my face. I sure didn't protest. "I thought I lost you, oh god," she said. "You're okay."

Once again, I hated my brother because he was married to this woman. But I was happy just the same that she cared and loved me this much. So I hugged her back. Then I collapsed into exhaustion.

Chapter 15

I SLEPT TO ABOUT 2:00 p.m. the next day. Brett was asleep in the spare bedroom, with Tika cuddled up next to her. I smiled at the two angels, as a mixture of red-and-blond hair spread out on the pillows they laid on. The paramedics had wrapped up Tika's left knee and had told her she had a slight sprain. But she would be fine after a few days' rest.

I got a Pepsi from the fridge and a red apple and went outside to the front steps. It was another sunny day, and I felt the sun warm my face as I ate my snack and glanced through a *Captain Lightning* comic.

Vinny came down the driveway shortly after drinking a Tang. He looked ten times worse than me. His eyes were red, and his left eye was black and blue. Vinny nodded at me and sat down beside me. We sat like that for a few moments, each lost in our thoughts.

Haywire had made it back to town and finally gotten Sheriff Foster to listen to his story, which was apparently confirmed by Parley Whitmore. Against the mayor's advice, Sheriff Foster rounded up a few men, and Brett insisted she was going along as well. As I said before, Penny's Creek was a small town, and news traveled pretty fast. Brett accompanied the party into the woods led by the town crazy.

After they found us, the sheriff went into the cave and came out shortly after, with the news of four confirmed dead; Officer Clinton Rushmore, Tim White, Anna Myers, and Johnny McDonald. The two latter were the bodies that we saw in the cave.

Clinton, being the one who was always leading the searches for the missing kids, was also in charge of the dogs that went searching for the missing kids in the woods of Penny's Creek. When they picked up the scent, Clinton easily ignored them and went on to another part of the woods. It could be weeks before anyone may find out how Clinton and Willy got together and committed the worst crimes our town ever had. Fat Willy was rushed to St. John's Bay medical center and was under twenty-four-hour guard. The missing kids were sent as well with their overjoyed families, including Andy and Kate who I hoped to visit very soon.

"That sure was messed up," Vinny said, simply.

"Sure was. Just glad it's over."

Sheriff Foster had told the group of us that we were all heroes. I didn't feel like one nor did I want to be called one. I was just looking for my missing friend, and somehow, the world went to crap Parley's father. A few days later, he was impeached for his incompetency, and he moved out of town shortly after. We never spoke with Parley since then. Parley went to do a great many things. He got a scholarship to Harvard and became an investment banker. He was killed instantly when the second airplane crashed into the World Trade Center on September 11, 2001.

"What do you want to do today?" Vinny asked.

We both looked at each other and said the same thing. "Sleep."

My parents came home that night and made a great dinner but drove me insane with the thousand times they asked if I was okay. Brett stayed over again, and we played Pitfall well into the night. She even tucked me in, which made me feel very young and silly but also kind of turned me on too.

"What's this doing under here?" my sister-in-law asked, kneeling down beside my bed. She pulled out the dream catcher. Brett sat down on the bed beside me and moved her gorgeous blond hair out of her face. "How come you have this under your bed?"

I had forgotten about the gift Sara gave me. "Hurt me much seeing it. But now…" I paused for a few seconds. "But seeing it now makes me feel good."

Brett nodded. "Little Sis. Tika sure did love that girl." She yawned. "Well, let's get some sleep. Shall I hang this back up?"

"Definitely."

She slipped the dream catcher back on the hook beside my bedroom window. She then leaned down and gave me a final hug. "Don't ever scare me like that again. I can't ever lose you."

I went to sleep content.

It was about 2:15 a.m. when I heard the closet door slowly open. *Oh no,* I thought. *Not tonight. Please not now.*

I heard the chain dragging on the wooden floor behind her. I slowly sat up, and Hazel was standing at the edge of my bed. Her white hair was done up in curlers, and her eyes had gone completely black. She twitched her head and spoke softly. "So you saved her and a couple of little shits. But you aren't safe, boy." She laughed her evil laugh. "Oh boy, you are so far from safe."

She began to swing the chain above her head like a lasso. The twirling noise it made seemed to fill the entire bedroom. "This time, I'm really going to hurt you." She ran her tongue over her cracked lips. "And you won't be waking up after it."

Suddenly, an orange light flashed into my bedroom. I turned, thinking it was a car light passing the house, but it was coming out of Sara's dream catcher. Suddenly, a human leg came out of the center of it, followed by another and then, an entire body.

It was impossible, but then again, there was an old, crazy lady whipping a chain in my bedroom.

"Get away from him, you toothless old bitch," Sara Foster said, standing beside my bed.

Hazel stopped swinging her chain and glared in fury at my friend.

I looked at Sara. She looked the same as she did the day she died; dressed in blue shorts, red T-shirt with Pat Benatar on it, and her Yankee hat. Cute, feisty, and brave; Sara Foster always was. "Don't worry, Morgan," she said, not taking her eyes of Hazel. "This woman isn't going to bother you ever again."

"Oh no?" Hazel said, moving slowly toward Sara. "Last time I checked, you were dead in the ground. A rotting fourteen-year-old corpse." She moved fast then swung the chain out toward Sara's face.

Sara grabbed Hazel's hand in an instant, twisted it, and bent it back. I heard Hazel's bones break, and she cried out in agony. Sara followed up with a punch, shattering the six teeth in the old woman's mouth. Blackish liquid poured of the woman's mouth.

"Go back to whatever dark cave you crawled out of!" Sara screamed.

She continued to punch and slap Hazel, moving her back toward the closet door. Hazel's face whipped back and forth, and she let out these low gurgles. "You will no longer bother him. You will no longer lay a finger on him."

Hazel tried to shove Sara back, but my friend was too strong. Again and again, Sara hit the woman. Hazel's face was filled with blood but not a drop of it landed on Sara. "Get back to hell, ugly!" Sara shouted, wrapping Hazel's chain around the woman's neck and kicking her back into the closet.

Hazel fell back into the darkness, her screams echoing from within, and then, she was gone. The closet door slowly shut on its own.

"She won't be back," Sara said, coming over and sitting Indian-style on the bed.

"I don't understand, Sara," I said. "You died."

I was scared, but I had to know for sure. My hand reached toward her, knowing my hand would pass right through her even though she held no ghostly form. But I felt her body instead.

"I am dead, Morgan," she said, gently holding my hand. She felt warm as if she was alive. She had that contagious smile that would always make another person smile back even if they were sad.

I didn't know what to say so I said, "Thank you."

"You saved Kate and those kids. I should thank you."

"I had a lot of help," I told her. "They miss you. I miss you, Sara."

"I miss you too, Morg," she said, gripping my hand tighter. "But I'm in a good place. I feel no pain, no sorrow. I'm happy."

"I'm glad," I told my best friend.

She slowly let go of me and got off the bed. She adjusted her Yankee hat and brushed her brown hair out of her eyes. "I have to get going now."

I moved off the bed and hugged my best friend one last time.

"You watch out for Christy for me?"

I nodded.

"Keep Vinny and Andy in check. Make sure Big Sis finds a good guy."

I felt her break the hug, and she moved back toward the dream catcher. "You are safe now."

"Will I ever see you again?" I asked, feeling my heart breaking again.

She smiled and touched my face gently. "I'll look in on you from time to time. I love you, Morgan O'Riely." A tear streamed down from her face.

"Love you, Sara Foster," I answered back. There was a bright orange flash again, and then, my best friend was gone.

I awoke a few seconds later. The room was still dark, but I no longer feared it. I never dreamed of Hazel again.

So that's the story of my spring/summer 1982. I made friends and lost friends. My life would never be the same without Sara. But I knew she would always be part of me just as Fat Willy, Tim, and even Haywire will. Life is hard and tough, but it's also wonderful and full of amazing stories and surprises.

Many other things happened to me in Penny's Creek. There was a time when my old friend, Tony Lombardo, moved back into town. I went on a trip to Florida with him and his family in a camper and the crap that happened to us on it was hilarious, and I still laugh about it to this day. There was also the time when Vinny swore there was a haunted house in the town, and he and Tika spent the night in it. There was also the time when Andy moved away to live in France. I have lots to tell you, but for now, I am content with just growing up in Penny's Creek.

About the Author

B OBBY ST. JOHN GREW up in a small town of Connecticut, where he still resides with his five children and his fiancé, Jenny. Many characters in his story are based on his real-life friends.